Lids Are Overrated

By Ellie Christina

To My Love,

Who Gave Me Time And Space.

To Those Who Inspired, Read, Helped Polish,

And Generally Supported Me.

Thank YOU

Chapter 1 – A 12 Hour Shift

VINNY'S ROADHOUSE. This curious little eatery has been planted on the same slab of concrete since before the road was a four-lane freeway. Built brand new, suffered and rundown, revamped, rundown again and now completely restored to its original vintage glory. Clean and classy, the interior shines. Polished floors with a hint of glitter and freshly rubbed ruby red vinyl seats. Stepping inside is to be transported to another time. A time filled with family road trips, genuine customer service, and the expectation of a waitress on roller skates. The small dining room will seat fifty travelers comfortably, sixty if hard pressed. The Roadhouse has never been brimming with people and many hope it never will as that would damage its charm. The pride and innocence of this little hole in the road town would be utterly crushed if their roadside diner ever filled to capacity.

Along with the Roadhouse, there are the other freeway-side staples that round out the gas-food-lodging requirements. The small fuel station that still requires you to walk in to pay. Bill has run the station for sixty years; he says people still stop, walk in and pay so why change things? The Beckett family owns and runs the more shabby than chic strip motel that boasts of "rooms with character." There's a special discount for the rooms that may or may not spring a leak if the weather is less than fair. Behind the freeway facing facade is the real town. The little man behind the heavy curtain. There reside a church, a school, a hardware store, and a small grocery interspersed with at least three bars and a few odds and end shops. The same families that run the businesses own the businesses and support each others' businesses. It's a circle of life is that is slowly dying. Of the kids that go to college most don't come back; rarely does the town draw in new residents. However, twenty-two year old Emily is just such a anomaly. They joke that this is where her car ran out of fuel and she didn't have any cash to fill it up. The irony, or tragedy, of it is that it doesn't fall too far from the truth. One day, almost a year ago, she came to the Roadhouse looking for work and shelter. A shadow hung over her and a history followed behind her. All the same, they welcomed her to their strange little family, eager to have a new face. She gratefully accepted the invitation to stay. Gradually she sloughed off the shadow and buried the history, though sometimes it does try to return to haunt her.

Everyday for twelve hours she serves. Primarily her patrons are professional drivers and haulers, but occasionally a lost businessman or family with kids will find themselves here for a rest and greasy meal. She greets them with sweetness in her voice, her freckled face flashes a smile, and her chocolate brown curls bounce freely. Twelve hours of wiping tables, refilling coffee and sharing banter with the road weary, the young waitress fleetly floats around the dining floor. The coffee is always hot, though it may not always be fresh, and the first cup is always free. Emily likes to believe the Roadhouse has a special something that draws in the consistent crowd. But more likely it is the sign that warns drivers that this is the very last gas, food or lodging for over a hundred miles in any direction.

~~~~~~~~~~~~~

A new morning; sunlight breaks through the smudgy front windows. Emily is bursting at the seams with giddy energy. Today she's tucked her burdens away and is a devout believer in new beginnings. Tomorrow may be different. With smooth grooves she moves around preparing for the breakfast crowd, or the dinner crowd, depending on the direction you're coming at the day. If you've been on the road all night, then this may be your last stop before hauling it in for some shut eye. Or this could be the caffeine stop that gets your morning started. Either way the coffee has been freshened, the grills are heated and the hands are ready to serve you the perfect bookend meal to your day.

Emily smiles, full of purpose and joy in serving, as the first of the big rigs pulls in. The bell on the door jingles a happy welcome. Emily looks the trucker over as he ambles in. He's dressed in the characteristic jeans and work boots, sporting a two day growth of beard. He looks tired but not beaten. Road hardened, as are most of the truckers that Emily meets.

"Morning, sir," she chimes. "Breakfast or dinner?" He smiles at the question.

"Well," he starts, "I guess I ought to be having dinner, but breakfast sure sounds nice." With a smile and sharp nod she tells him to sit wherever he would like. Before he can fully take a seat

Emily promptly meets him there with a mug and some coffee.

"Decaf?" she asks before she pours just to be sure. He nods gratefully and welcomes the steaming cup of joe. Notepad at the ready Emily tells him about all the specials and options. After she jots down his order she twirls and floats toward the kitchen window to deliver it. Her curls spring and bounce with every flowing step.

"Morning, Harry!" she calls into the kitchen and clips up the order on the carousel. Harry, a fifty-something biker turned short order cook, waves to her. His long gray hair is pulled back into a wavy ponytail and covered with bandana, his beard carefully tucked into a hair net. Under a greasy white apron he wears a crisp white t-shirt. The edges of some aged tattoos slip out from beneath the short sleeves.

"Morning, Honey," he calls back. His voice is gruff from years of abuse, but his demeanor is sweet and safe.

"Caroline here yet?" Emily inquires.

"Yes she is!" comes a voice from the backdoor. Caroline, Harry's wife and business partner, comes in with an armload of paperwork and assorted office clutter.

"Morning, Caroline!" Emily hurries to help with the load. Caroline is happy to hand over all she's carrying. Emily bluffs buckling under the weight, laughs a little, then carries it off to the utility closet/office.

"Ugh, she's chipper, again," Caroline says and makes a face.

"Yes she is," says Harry, solid and genuine. "And that's a

good thing." Caroline groans with mock disgust. Harry marches over to Caroline, and gently kisses her cheek.

"Aww." Emily sighs with amusement, as she comes back from the office.

Caroline pushes Harry away; he in turn smacks her rear end. "Get your apron woman! People are hungry, time to feed 'em!" Though she owns and runs the diner she still serves part time as a waitress. Caroline feigns excitement; Emily stifles a giggle.

The waitresses take up their posts, answering the calls for coffee and sustenance. Emily answers with sweet energy, Caroline with salty quips. With the energy starting to fill the room, a young family comes in. A Mom and Dad, Son and Daughter. Almost like a perfect storybook family, but not quite. The two kids look like they've completely sucked the energy from their parents, boiled it with pure adrenaline and shot it directly into their own veins. Mom and Dad look bedraggled and in desperate need to regain some of the stolen liveliness.

"Good Morning, folks. Have a seat wherever you'd like, and I'll be right with you!" Emily calls and waves. The parents acknowledge her as the children quickly direct them where to sit. Too weak to fight, they follow their kids' wishes. The boy jumps on the seat and encourages his sister to follow suit. The parents do their level best to contain the little hooligans. Emily hurries over to get in the middle and hopefully distract the young ones from more terrorist activities, thinking the whole way that the roadhouse would benefit from children's menus, or maybe straightjackets.

"What can I get for you today?" Emily says cheerfully while agilely blocking a straw paper shot by one of the pumped up children.

"Coffee," both parents say in perfect, languished harmony.

"Can do," Emily says as she jots it down. "Anything for the kiddos?"

The Father looks to the Mother; she stares blankly back at him.

"Hot cocoa!" shout the kids as they begin jumping again. Horror flashes across Emily's face as visions of burn treatments and EMTs dance in her head. Not to mention the sticky clean up. Lighting off some napalm would yield less of a mess than the explosive energy of these kids.

"No, I don't think so," Mom answers.

Phew. Yay, Mom.

"Orange juice, I guess," Dad says finally. He looks to Mom but she's too busy getting Son and Daughter to sit down again to agree or disagree. So Dad nods again and says that'll do. Emily forces a smile. Better, still sticky, but won't require calling 911 for a scalded child.

"You want lids on the juices?" she asks hopefully. Both parents nod vigorously as the kids again climb up on the seats and begin to jump and laugh. Emily's eyes widen and she decides it's best to walk away. With a quick twirl and skip she's halfway to the kitchen. Caroline watches the booth with squinted eyes and skepticism. She murmurs about some peoples' kids.

"They ordered them juice too didn't they?"

Emily nods affirmatively.

Caroline scowls. "Your table, your mess."

"Uh," Emily hesitates, but convinces herself that the sense of foreboding is exaggerated. "Don't worry, everything will be fine." She almost believes it. Caroline on the other hand walks away shaking her head. Emily quickly pulls the drinks together and makes her way to deliver them. The kids continue to bounce. As the young waitress gets closer, the sense of dread only deepens. No turning back now. With polished skill she balances the juices on the tray and begins to pour the coffee. Dad's eyes light up as the hope of hot caffeine fills him, but it's not to last. One of the kids jumps at the worst possible moment and knocks the tray from Emily's carefully balanced grip. In slow motion horror, a steaming pot of coffee and two chilly glasses of orange juice go flying up and crashing down. The whole world seems to gasp. Mom leans in, as if somehow hoping she can help this young lady magically save the day; Dad leans away knowing full well there's no way she can. Emily cringes. Waiting. With a crash and a whoosh of liquid everything finally comes to a rest on the table, floor, and the now soaked server. All are completely still for a moment, totally dumbfounded. Even the kids are still, gaping expressions of fear and awe frozen on their faces. The parts of Emily's arm that were scalded by the hot coffee have since been nicely doused by the cold juice. Lids on the juice?

Nice idea, but altogether proven pointless. The place is steeped in stunned silence. Caroline watches, unaffected by the disaster, with an I-told-you-so look on her face. There's almost a hint of a smile, but she's not that cruel. The Dad looks in front of him. One cup of coffee, still righted, the holy grail of his morning. He less than discreetly picks it up and takes a deep swallow. Emily and the Mom both shoot him the look of death. He sets the cup down and looks away sheepishly. Caroline sighs, then shouts toward to the kitchen, "Harry! Get the mop bucket!"

The family of mayhem manages to eat their meal with relatively few additional incidents and leaves a large tip for their long suffering waitress. The chaos continues for awhile with barely a break to mop up the messes. But the hustle abruptly sinks into a quiet depression of twiddling thumbs and heaving sighs. The coffee pots that earlier could not be kept full now sit in a stale simmer, the brew slowly turning into a dark sludge that many expect from diners like this. Emily has taken a moment to change clothes, don a fresh apron and a new smile. The day continues to ebb and flow; rampant pandemonium morphs into utter silence thick with boredom. The bipolar vacillation is either perfectly timed to give the hard working three man crew a well deserved break, or to drive them completely mad with the inconsistency. Notwithstanding they are forced to endure. Burgers and fries, hotcakes and hash browns. Roadies and travelers fed and restored to traveling condition. Eventually dusk does come and embraces the small diner. The nearby freeway looks less like moving cars and more like fireflies careening past. The drone of the tires and the whoosh of their passing is a lullaby to the vanishing sunlight.

Emily cruises around the dining room, her last burst of energy for the last ninety minutes of her twelve hour shift. She continues floating between tables and spot wiping them as she goes. It's busy work, as the room is nearly empty. Only a single, lonely figure sits in a back booth. A young woman. Old college hoodie pulled over her head. Looking a bit worse for the wear, the isolated woman stares downcast at the table. She seems to be in her twenties or thirties, but carries a further age that doesn't come so much with time as it does with events. Emily can identify. Several locks of hair rebelliously fall around the woman's face. The locks are jet black; one, though, is blue. Blue like her expression and whole demeanor. Emily arrives next to her table bearing coffee and pleasant greetings. The Blue Girl acknowledges her presence without looking up. She's been crying. Emily is instantly sympathetic.

"Hi there. Coffee?" Emily sets the mug down.

The young woman shakes her head "Oh, no. I can't pay... "

Emily smiles. "First cup is on the house." She pours the hot liquid. A breath of relief comes from the morose figure. Even this stale sludge can brighten an evening for someone in need. The vaguest hint of a smile appears on the corners of her mouth.

"Hang on a minute and I'll get you something to eat." The woman looks up, worried. Her dark brown eyes are bloodshot and bear dark circles. Emily reassures her that there will be no charge and that it's just extra food that needs to be eaten. Blue Girl nods with reluctant agreement; Emily nod back and hurries to the kitchen.

"Harry, I need a favor." Harry looks up. He's cleaning the griddles, again. His eyes meet Emily's.

"What's up, honey?"

She tells Harry about the Blue Girl, and slowly admits that she's promised her a free meal. Harry smiles.

"That's awful sweet of you. Let me see what I can pull together for her. I think I've got just the thing." Harry shakes his finger at her as he thinks and starts to move around the kitchen and various food stores. The waitress' eyes sparkle as she watches him. Harry comes back with some treasures and together they plate up a wonderful meal. Emily looks their masterpiece over.

"Thanks Harry," Emily says with deepest sincerity. "It means a lot to me."

Harry nods knowingly. "It's good of you."

Emily whisks the plate away and takes it to the Blue Girl. She gently sets the meal down. The woman freezes as she looks at the gift in front of her. Is that a tear? Blue Girl looks up at Emily and smiles gratefully, but seems afraid to eat. Emily takes a step back.

"I'll check on you in a while, okay?" she says, then twirls off to answer the call of a couple of truckers in need of some caffeine to get them through the night. More stragglers come through the door so that Emily can barely manage a glance and quick "how you doing" to the Blue Girl, let alone learn more about her or make sure she's really okay. Emily feels stretched as if she is somehow tethered to this figure in the corner booth. Every distraction rips and pulls her apart. The disturbances are endless.

Finally free for a minute, she goes to grab the Blue Girl's empty plate. As she approaches she sees the woman is on a cell phone. Her countenance has dropped again as have the tears. "What? Are you kidding me?" A long pause. Blue Girl's face contorts in anger then drops into defeat and disappointment. "No. No, that's fine." Emily watches with worry, but realizing the need for privacy, she takes her plate and slowly steps away. With a stolen glance back Emily sees Blue Girl bitterly throw her phone into her bag and bury her face in her hands. Thoughts racing, what should she do? Can she help or would that be invading? Caroline calls for Emily to meet some truckers at the cash register. Then it's off to clear more dishes, take orders, wipe down tables. Again. Use, wash, repeat. Over and over. The shift is truly grating on her now. Eventually she can take a breath, and looks to the booth. But the lone figure is gone. The booth is now occupied by another group.

"Caroline, where did she go?" Emily inquires with urgency and force that she neither intended nor expected. Caroline is taken aback.

"Where did who go?"

Emily gestures to the booth. Caroline nods. "She slipped out after some truckers. Hitching a ride no doubt." Emily sinks into her thoughts, feeling the weight of a missed opportunity.

"She left some things behind too. I put them in the box," Caroline throws out as a sidenote.

Emily hurries behind the counter where on a shelf tucked away is a box. Harry's sloppy handwritten "Stuff I Found" marks it as a place to put all the peculiar things that customers leave behind. Backtracking is not a commonly accepted practice of road warriors. If you are careless enough to leave it in a highway cafe, you can probably live without it. Or didn't really need it in the first place. Emily begins to paw through the assortment of oddities. Sunglasses, ball cap, pink pocket knife, a tin of mints... why didn't they just throw that away? And what's this, a book? A darkly bound faux leather journal, that's new. Emily grips the book tightly and fingers the cover a moment. She opens the front jacket. This Book Belongs To: is left blank. No name or contact information. No clue at all. Front to back, top to bottom, flipping through the pages filled with writing and sketches she is careful not to read any of the entries. Well, maybe she'll come back, or call, or send someone to retrieve it. Such a personal object, she would want it back... wouldn't she?

Chapter 2 - Carpe Diem

THE BELL RINGS. Somehow with it comes a deep sense of foreboding. Something is coming that will taint the whole day, or maybe it's Publisher's Clearing House with a handful of balloons and a giant check. No, it's the former. A pause for suspense is followed by the clatter, laughter and noise that one would expect to accompany a winning football team or a rock band followed by about fifty groupies. The new decibel level is mind boggling. Emily looks to see a group of about eight teenagers. Road trippers. They look like high school seniors that are trying to make their mark. Why'd they have to pick this diner? With a quick nod for a greeting she tells them to have a seat. She slowly starts to get a pitcher of water, all the while looking for some way to avoid going to their table.

The bell rings again. A Mom and her Little Girl walk in slowly. If people actually turn green when they're feeling sick, this little girl is very green indeed. Shaky and in a cold sweat, the poor thing looks miserable. The asphalt is cruel, to some more than others. For this innocent traveler, the road has proved too much. Caroline comes out from the back and begins to survey the situation. Emily's eyes light up.

"I'll take the sick little girl if you take the teens," she spouts speedily. Caroline looks her over, dubious, but agreeable. Emily beams with relief and hands off the water pitcher.

"Tips go to whoever doesn't need the mop bucket for their

table," Caroline says in a hushed speakeasy voice.

"You're on," Emily answers, confident she can help cure what ails the child, and knowing full well the teens could have extremely explosive eating habits.

Emily gathers a few aids: a cool damp rag, some soda water and salted crackers. She arranges them nicely on a tray and pours a coffee for the Mom. Meanwhile, armed with tenacity and experience, Caroline marches over to the teens. They're totally absorbed in their adventure and have no idea Caroline is there. Emily again breathes a sigh of relief, grateful they're no longer her responsibility.

"Hi there," Emily says, almost in a whisper. The Mom has her arms wrapped around her daughter. Emily sets the tray down. "I brought a few things that I thought might help." Thankfulness glows in the Mom's face.

"Let me know if you need anything else," Emily says, then covertly whispers to the mom where the bathroom is in case worse comes to worst. Motion sickness is a common malady seen at the diner. The illness comes in many forms, from queasy tummies and headaches to plain old jangled nerves. Everyone handles it differently, and no one is immune. Even the strongest road warriors are sometimes struck. The simple fact is that sometimes the road wins.

Emily walks past Caroline and the teens as she returns to the kitchen.

"Young man, pull up your pants. It's too early for the moon

to be out," Caroline quips coldly. The teens all laugh at the target of her remark. One of them belly laughs, then snorts. The entire group erupts in heartier laughter and over the top giggles.

Once the teens have their food and all the tables are content for the time being, Emily carries on with busy work behind the counter. Caroline stops next to her. The young waitress suddenly feels cornered and senses a threat of confrontation. Oh bother. Caroline stares at her. Relentless. Emily's shoulders shrivel after a moment of the pressure. Finally she bursts.

"What?!"

"Why are you so eager to avoid the rabble over there?" Caroline smiles slightly as she inquires. A long awkward moment passes. Emily bides her time and uses her fingernail to chip something sticky off the counter.

"Teens... they're unpredictable," she starts. "Like, are they gonna try hard in school and help old ladies cross the street? Or get up in your face and yell strange things at you, or throw eggs at your garage?" Boggled, Caroline stares at her associate like she's been painted blue and grown a third ear. She rubs her temples as if fending off a headache. Emily heaves a sigh and looks for something else to do, anywhere.

"You're, what? Twenty?" Caroline ventures.

"Twenty-two," Emily corrects.

"It really hasn't been that long since you were a teenager."

Emily groans at the thought. "No. I was never--"

"Never what? Never a teen? Did you just skip those years,

went from age twelve right to twenty-two?"

"No, I was just never like them. I didn't fit in as a teen." Emily looks away ashamedly.

"This may come as a surprise to you, but no one fits in as a teenager. That's kind of the whole point of being a teen. Not fitting in, and figuring out how to." Another long silence envelopes them. Caroline is oddly cool with it. Emily can only assume she enjoys causing the discomfort and watching her victim squirm. Finally, again, the pressure builds to unbearable levels. Emily is mere seconds away from baring her soul when one of the youths hollers over for Caroline. Saved by the teen. How ironic. Left to her own thoughts Emily wonders what exactly it is that frightens her so much about these kids. They're harmless, or at least mostly harmless. She has four years of age and experience on them. Experience, maybe that is the problem. The teens in front of her now are cool and confident, everything that she wanted to be and wasn't. Even as a young adult she feels inadequate next to them. This is stupid, they're kids. They probably feel just as self conscious and uncertain as she does. Nah, probably not.

Most of the dining room is empty again. The Little Girl recovered, shared a light meal with her mom and left a much more human shade of pink. Emily smiles with pride, knowing she aided in helping a child feel better as well as not requiring the mop bucket. The table of teens has been silenced, at least from talking, since their food was delivered. No mop bucket for them either, yet. Taking a quiet moment, Emily leans against the bar by the cash register and postcards. Mindlessly she fingers the license plate shaped keychains. Carpe Diem, one reads. Emily makes a face at the thought. Latin baloney. She had tried to take on great things in her life but they all blew up in her face. Love, education, career. Her lovers destroyed her, colleges rejected her, and careers escaped her. Destiny hated her and she was done trying. Taking care of road trippers, truckers, and carsick kids was gonna be her lot now. Maybe that's not such a bad lot. But just maybe...

"Hellooooo!" Emily is jolted from her thoughts. The teens stand at the counter ready to pay the check. The mercy is that they are ready to leave, the pity is that Emily happens to be the one at the cash register. Suck it up, girl, just get them out the door. She marshals her sweetest most genuine smile for the group.

"How was your meal?"

"Great, yeah," one of the boys says with a deep swagger. He's probably the oldest, and quite possibly the alpha male of the group. Emily can't tell if he's showing off for her specifically, or the entire room. Either way his presentation of prowess is seeping out of his skin along with the caustic stench of his bad cologne. He lays out a wad of cash and a handful of coins. "I think that'll cover it." Emily fakes a smile. Don't make me touch it. Fearful of what she will find intermingled with it, she carefully picks through the payment. Lint, gum wrapper, old grocery receipt. Phew, it could've been worse. It has been. She separates the non-cash items; flattening and organizing the bills as she counts it all out. She pauses a moment, looks at the check again and slides him a dollar and a few coins back. "Too much," she says quietly.

The boy smiles "Heh, thanks." He says.

"Hey we got enough for a tip!" another teen chimes in. There's a brief and raucous cheer. Emily's smile is so forced now, it hurts her face. "Great, I'll make sure your server gets it." A whole buck, eighty-five. Wow, that'll make Caroline's day.

A couple of the girls stand near the tacky tokens and souvenirs. Mr. Alpha calls to them that it's time to go.

"Just a sec. I'll be right out," one girl answers. She is cute and skinny, too skinny. Long legs and perfectly placed ponytail, she looks like a cheerleader. Her name is probably Tiffany, or Pepper. She, another girl and one of the guys stay behind while all the others go out to the cars. The other girl wears glasses, but they're not just geeky glasses. They're the kind that make you look smart and cool. Emily is pretty sure they didn't make those when she was in school. The boy that decided to stay with them is a scraggly beanpole of a kid. Scruffy hair and baggy clothes that hang long on his narrow frame. Trouble, yeah, he looks like trouble.

A conversation starts that makes Emily cringe. They're trying to read Latin.

"What does Crap Dime mean?" Baggy Britches asks snidely.

The young waitress wills herself to disappear.

"Car-pe Di-em. It's Latin. Means something like seize the day," Emily says forcefully.

The annoying boy laughs again. "Seizure day?" He snorts and pretends, with no skill, to have a seizure, limbs shaking, tongue hanging out like a dog. The Cheerleader, who had first shown interest in the keychains, fists him hard in the shoulder and yells at him for being stupid. Emily finds herself smiling slightly and silently cheering for the girl. The boy grabs his shoulder and winces in pain. He gives her an ugly look, then comments that he'll be outside. He barges through the door as if trying to make a statement of his rage. It's reminiscent of a three year old when his daddy doesn't buy him the milkshake he wanted. But less cute.

"Seize the day? What does that mean?" The Cheerleader asks, turning back to the subject at hand. She and her friend are both genuinely interested. Emily is relieved to answer a sincere question.

"Take every advantage of the time you have. Live in the moment."

"Wow, cool. I love that! Sarah, isn't that cool?" Sarah pushes her glasses up and shrugs; her interest lost. She pulls her phone out and begins texting. The Cheerleader doesn't waver or lose momentum. She looks at Emily since Sarah's not really listening to her anymore. "That's so perfect. We all decided to go on this road trip together so we could do just that. Live in the moment, I mean. I mean we're just about done with high school and we're gonna be leaving for college and getting real jobs. Carpe Diem, that's totally my new motto."

Emily flashes another smile. Oh wow, she just picked a whole new motto based on a key chain in a diner. The Cheerleader buys the trinket and hooks it to her purse.

"I love it," she shows it to Sarah, her expression begging her friend to comment on it.

"No, yeah it's cool." Sarah nods then nudges her friend toward the door. "It's time to go."

"Oh! Right." The Cheerleader snaps to and quickly makes for the exit. She hollers a quick thank you as they go out the door. The diner plunges into silence. In that instant Emily relaxes. Until the bell falls off the door. The noise is hideous as it clatters to the floor and brings all the tensions back to the surface. Emily shudders, a twinge of jealousy accompanying the stress. Why didn't someone tell her to do this kind of thing a few years ago, before she made all the terrible choices that led her to all the wrong places? Her version of this road trip was too little too late. It ended in a empty little town and dinky diner.

"Carpe Diem, my --" Emily looks up. Harry stands in front of her; she bites her lips. He scratches his hair-netted beard.

"Em, you okay?" she indicates that she is not. Harry doesn't budge; in fact he seems to settle in. He breathes a deep gravelly sigh and leans against the counter. Such a presence would normally set her on edge, but she feels her guard slowly slipping.

Fine, he wants to know.

"Little Miss Teeny Bopper thinks she's an instant scholar/philosopher just because she bought an overpriced geegaw at a Podunk truckstop. 'Oh, wow, it's Latin, that makes me smart, I'll make that my personal motto'" Emily mimics dramatically. Harry nods a moment, taking in what she said. Then the gesture changes from understanding to disagreement.

"That ain't it. That ain't it at all." Emily looks at him, shocked, puzzled, then almost fearful. There's something knowing in his eyes. Her expression begs him not to press it any further.   Without words he agrees and meanders back to the kitchen. Caroline passes him in the hallway. Harry smacks her on the rear end making her jump and squeal. He laughs heartily and maniacally.

Befuddled at this strange ritual, Emily finds herself smiling in spite of herself.

"Oh, Caroline, those kids left you a tip." Emily hands Caroline the money.   "There's some assorted pocket litter to go with it, if you want. You know, sentimental reasons, maybe?"

"Um, no. Thank you." Caroline looks at the sad amount and fingers the coins a little.

"I wouldn't touch it any more than you have to." Emily says with no small amount of pleasure. Caroline makes a face and drops the new wealth into her apron pocket. A moment passes. Caroline looks expectantly at Emily.

"What about your little girl, did she require anything from the supply closet?"

"Neither mop, nor bucket was required," Emily says proudly.

"Then it seems to be a draw. Were you tipped well?"

Emily sinks a little. Caroline asks if they tipped at all.

"Not a drop."

"Pity." Caroline is less than sympathetic; her tip may be more of an insult but at least she received one. Emily is done with the conversation and leaves the room to find something else to do. The remainder of her shift runs by as one might expect. She spends the time serving quickly and avoiding deep conversations with her coworkers.

By the end of her shift her clothes bear an eclectic array of smears and stains. Like the Illustrated Man, her body tells the many stories of mishaps and calamitous adventures in food service and dining. She retreats to the break room to change and stuffs the dirty duds into her backpack.

"Emily, honey!" Caroline's boisterous voice calls from the front door. "Your boyfriend is here to walk you safely home!" Emily rolls her eyes. That would be Dom, the handsome young man who runs the hardware store with his dad. He has made it his mission to make sure Emily is safely escorted back to the motel where she is still living. Emily often questions whether he just wants to walk her home. What is this, the nineteen-forties? Who still does this? She sometimes wonders if this little town isn't caught in a time warp. Or maybe it's simply a tradition that gets handed down in small communities like this. She still can't decide if the practice is really strange or really wonderful. Either way, Emily has convinced herself she neither wants nor needs this kind of attention. She's just getting herself straight again; a love interest is not on her to-do list. Though she can't deny that she enjoys having a friendship with someone her own age.

"Hey Dom," she calls as she comes out to join them. His eyes light up when he sees her. Uh-oh, maybe someone needs to tell him there's nothing romantic going on.

"Ready?" Dom asks as he holds the door open for her. She musters a little extra life and answers that she is very ready to go home. Dom dashingly takes the backpack from her and slings it over his own shoulder. They all share goodnight salutations and step out into the night. The fresh outdoor air is a welcome relief.

"So nice to smell something that's not deep fried," she tells him as she grabs her bike. The two-wheeler is a vintage blue cruiser complete with white banana seat and a wicker basket on the handle bars. She picked it up at a yard sale shortly after she decided to stay in town. The bike was in like new condition, further confirmation of the time warp that is this whistle-stop.

The two begin an easy stroll home. They walk without speaking for a few moments with the sounds of a few crickets and the bike tires crackling along the gravel following them, and the freeway's ever present hum falling farther into the background.

"So, you're a hardware guy," Emily starts.

"Yes, I'm often told that."

"My bell fell off today." The statement falls flat. Dom

snickers a little. "The bell off the door. Where is your mind!" She pushes him away a little. She cringes to herself, realizing how flirtatious that felt. Dom raises his hands in surrender.

"Sorry, sorry. Just sounded... funny. So, what do you need to fix it?"

"I don't know, I got it back up tonight, but I don't know how long it'll last."

"Okay," Dom says matter-of-factly. "I'll bring some goodies over and we'll see what can be done. It is an old rig, it might just be time for a new one."

Emily looks at him in shock. "No way. I'm not going to just replace it. Not giving up that easy." How dare he try to replace a perfectly good bell.

"Okay. Fair enough," Dom says, trying to appease. "I'll bring stuff by in the next day or so, and we'll see what we can do." She smiles, but her expression fades. They've reached the Becket's motel. Emily fishes the key out of her pocket.

"Well, goodnight. Thanks for walking me." She swiftly unlocks the door and parks the bike inside. Dom smiles at her. Oh no. Just go home, please. Her thoughts show in her face as he quickly backs away.

"Yeah," he hesitates but surrenders. "Goodnight, then." He turns and walks away. Emily abruptly waves and shuts the door behind her. A quiver goes down her spine. Carpe Diem can stuff it.

Chapter 3 – Stuff I Found

Morning dawns. Full of the possibility, Emily rides her cruiser through town. The waking sun gradually burns away the morning fog. The crisp spring air smells fresh, but still has a frosty bite to it. The little neighborhood slowly shakes off the sleep and prepares for the new day. Open signs are placed or illuminated. Crystal clean doors and windows glisten in the sunlight. Though this small world is old and worn, it somehow carries airs of being fresh and new. What a funny place. Lost in the jumble of on and off ramps, a little refuge for the weary. An oasis in the desert of everyday chaos. Slow, quiet, peaceful. Thoughts that twelve months ago would have made Emily shudder, but now she finds them to be a deep, cleansing breath. What once she saw as a prison, now she sees as a shelter. But how long should she stay and hide?

She eases to a stop in front of the roadhouse. Ugh, those windows are filthy, something should be done about that. There's a feeling of some affection, and maybe even pity, for the little diner. She leans the bike against the building next to the large front window. No extra precaution, chains or padlocks required. As she comes inside, she follows the sound of casual disagreement coming from the kitchen. Tsk, tsk, they're at it again. She peers into the kitchen to see Harry gesture with spatula in his hand, waving it around to make his point. Caroline stands with hands on hips. Her silence is speaking volumes.

Emily sometimes wonders if their arguments are more like sports than actual disagreements. Maybe they carry on to keep their minds sharp and fend off the repetitiveness of their lives. Either way, the feud quickly comes to an end as Caroline throws up her hands.

"Fine. Have it your way," she states and motions to the griddle. "Just don't burn the hash browns, again!"

"Yeah, yeah. I've got it under control." Harry says. His voice is perfectly calm, there's even a hint that he's enjoying this. It's a game, to Harry anyway. Caroline scowls and storms out.

"Does that mean you won?" Emily inquires of Harry.

He laughs heartily. "There's no winning an argument with Caroline. Either you lose, or you really lose." Emily knows Caroline well enough to imagine it's true. Her strong personality would be hard to combat and even harder to prove wrong.

"Does it ever get-" Emily pauses, hesitant to take the conversation to anything deeper. Harry encourages her to ask her question. "Does it ever get too serious, like you guys might be in trouble?"

"I'm in trouble everyday." Harry laughs but sees the seriousness in Emily's expression. "Sure, we've had our share of bumps in the road," Harry answers honestly. "They make things rock and rattle, but it's the test that proves how strong we are actually put together. If there was love there to begin with, trouble makes it stronger."

"Hmm." She grows distant, carried away by unwelcome

memories. Trouble never did anything to make her relationships stronger. Harry places his hands on her shoulders. "Any relationship requires maintenance if you want it to last," he says. "When something breaks, you duct tape and baling twine the thing back together. It doesn't matter what fails. Punctured tires or snapped belts."

"The snapped belts are usually due to the spare tires, aren't they?" Caroline cackles from the storage closet. Emily's eyebrows shoot up and she stifles a laugh.

"Hey, woman! I'm imparting wisdom here!" He waves her off. "Besides," he leans in and whispers to Emily, "have enough flat tires on the road you learn it's good to always carry a spare." He proudly pats his front side. Emily giggles, her sparkle gradually coming back to the surface. Harry flips the hash browns on the griddle and pokes them a couple of extra times.

The bell jingles on the front door. Emily jumps and spins and leaps away, all in one beautiful and fluid movement. Harry follows her with his gaze. His concern and his curiosity are quelled at the smell of burning hash browns. He exclaims and quickly removes them from the heat.

The bell jingles again, but the sound is followed by a horrible clattering as it plummets and bounces across the floor. The ruckus sounds as much like "ouch" as a bell could possibly ever muster. Two times in as many days. This does not bode well. The few guests have found their seats and contently gaze at the single page menus, so Emily takes it upon herself to rescue the bell. She plucks the sad little ringer from the floor, climbs up on a chair and takes a moment to examine the problem. With a little fiddling here and bending there she gets the pieces back together. She hops down carefully, watching it skeptically. It's not pretty, but it'll hold for now. She turns her eyes to the large window. Smears and grime announce its sad neglect. How long has it been since it was washed? Her contemplation is cut short as customers soon call for her attention.

The roadhouse grows busier; Emily and Caroline must strive to keep up with the steady stream of diners. The approaches and mannerisms of the two spirited servants are drastically different. Where Emily is fleet of foot and floats from table to table with rhythm and poise, Caroline marches to her own beat and stomps out a cadence of efficiency. Together there is music in their movements, a rare and eccentric harmony that keeps the diner from falling into disarray.

"You know this salted caramel flavor craze?" A Trucker asks as he stops to pay his check. "The two of you are like that. Salt and caramel."

Caroline laughs. "Sounds messy to me." The Trucker throws some cash down on the counter; it's a fifty-dollar bill. Caroline rolls her eyes. "Gee, got anything bigger? Want me to break it into singles?" Caroline doesn't expect an answer, and simply begins to work the cash register.

The Trucker points to Emily. "She's the caramel," he says with a wink. Emily feels a rush of heat flush her cheeks and finds herself smiling timidly.

Caroline mockingly glares at the Trucker. "Yeah, she'll give you a toothache."

The Trucker laughs deeply. Caroline finishes ringing him up and slides him the change, but he holds up his hand refusing to take it. He slides it back with a quick nod and another wink. Caroline returns the nod with a genuine smile of gratitude. So much spoken without words, Emily notices. Another of those old fashioned things about this little world she's found herself in.

~~~~~~~~~~

Emily hums and twirls toward the window, rag and spray cleaner in hand. A few contented patrons enjoy their meals, shakes and java. Some smile as they covertly watch. The spritely waitress inadvertently entertains the entire room of weary travelers. She pulls a chair up to the large front window and takes to washing it, humming some unknown tune to herself as she swipes and scrubs away the dust, muck and fingerprints. Soon the window is glistening. The sunlight that once was muted by the thick layer of filth, now streams through unhindered. Satisfied, Emily stows her rag in her back pocket and hooks the bottle of blue liquid over her apron waistband as if holstering a weapon. The solution sloshes back and forth with the motion of her hips as she grooves to the beat inside her head. Pulling a window marker from another pocket she, with grace and contemplation, creates large loose letters on the window. The writing declares a welcome and invitation to come enjoy the food.

To entice prospective customers further she writes out the special of the day. Two pancakes, two eggs, and hash browns for one low and sensible price. She hops down and examines the writing.

"Harry! What do you think?" Emily calls. Harry comes out, wiping his hands on a towel which he then slings over his shoulder. He looks at the words on the window. He smiles and nods, but gradually gets a confused look on his face. Emily is worried.

"What's wrong?" she asks

"It's backward," he answers. Emily laughs.

"You can read it on the outside." Harry's eyes light up. He goes outside to read it. Emily laughs as do several other customers who have continued to watch. Harry comes back inside and nods approvingly.

"That's a talent," he says matter of factly.

"I'm dyslexic, I do it on accident sometimes." Emily shrugs. At least now she had use for the ability.

A modern silver sedan pulls into the gravel parking lot, quickly followed by an old beater station wagon, a nineteen-nineties suburban and a bright red convertible. They appear to be traveling in one of the most heterogeneous caravans Emily has ever seen. Harry looks at Emily in awe.

"It's working already!" He pats her shoulder and makes his way back to the kitchen.

Each vehicle seems to be filled to capacity with passengers and gear. The people are more eccentric than the cars they came in. Some wear suits and ties, some look like they're preparing to go on walkabout, some chic, some less so. They all file in together, talking, laughing, and carrying on as if they've known each other for years. Emily tries not to stare, but the group is fascinating. Eventually she snaps herself out of the daze and steps out to greet the collective.

"Hey there. Go ahead and have a seat wherever and I'll be around with some water in a minute." The crowd erupts in murmured agreements and thanks. They slowly spread out to the various seats. Some pull tables together, others find places of relative solitude. A young man, a geeky science type with the latest smartphone and laptop, sits next to a cute hippie chick with a pencil and notepad made from recycled materials. Emily realizes this is a huge undertaking that may require backup. She hurries to the kitchen window and calls to Harry.

"Hey, where's Caroline?" Harry shrugs at first then remembers. He tells Emily that she's running errands and then was going to call it a day. "She figured you had it all under control here. She has faith in you."

Great. Why'd she have to get so trusting all of a sudden? Emily rolls her shoulders and gets down to business. She fills and delivers water pitchers and cups, and takes orders for other drinks.

As she hurries to serve for the large crew she picks up snippets of their conversation, but only comes away confused. It seems so random and disjointed.

"So," she starts, but wishes she didn't have to ask. "How

many checks will we need?" The individuals all look around at each other. There's clearly no real leader to this band of misfits. The discussion varies from everyone getting a separate check, to getting two checks, one for guys and one for girls, or maybe they should be in groups of three. Emily desires only to slip away and give them another minute to figure it out. But they reach a consensus on having one single check for their poor waitress to keep track of. A few apologize and promise to be easier in the future. Others are less sympathetic. It's going to be a long evening.

The banter back and forth saturates the diner. Once everyone is settled, Emily inquires where they are all going together. They perk up at her interest, but seem a little hesitant to volunteer any information.

"It's a crop circle," the Science Geek finally interjects.

Emily smiles. It's a joke, right? Where's the hidden camera? They convince her it's no gag, and jump right in to inviting her to join them. Ha, they really are nuts. Her desire quickly turns to feeding this group of crazies and sending them blithely on their way, but something in her stops. Is she actually contemplating it? No, not really. But it does stir her hunger for adventure, as well as the fear that holds her in place.

When the time comes for them to continue on their way, they all work to pool the right amount of money for their individual orders, and make sure she is well tipped. They begin to file out the door to their respective vehicles. Energetic banter continues the whole way.

"You really are welcome to join us, anytime," says the Hippie Chick before leaving. "Most of us have jobs. We just take some vacation time or a weekend for our excursions, then back home." She hands Emily a business card and points to the Science Geek. "It's his card, but you can reach any of us through him."

"Great." Emily takes the card with a polite smile. Great. I'm all for adventure, but crop circles? Takes all kinds.

The evening crawls along once the large crowd leaves. For some reason the monotony of this little world begins to pile up and become stifling. She had thought maybe this could be the last new job she would take for awhile, but in this moment it seems interminable. Is she completely stuck in this one horse town? Is that such a bad thing? She learned long ago this place lacked the social interaction she had gotten used to in the bigger cities, but maybe that wasn't bad; it kept her out of the kind of trouble she was also very familiar with. Her mind wanders to Dom. She seems to have traded in a bar hopping, hot dancing nightlife for a young man who is content just to walk her home. How quaint. How boring. How sweet, safe, and honest.

Emily continues to be lost in thought as she wipes off tables. She works her cleaning routine around the dining room and to the counters. Behind the counters she begins to straighten the shelves. Various clutter is found here. Old menus, extra cleaning supplies and...a box. The "Stuff I Found" box. Why couldn't Harry call it a lost and found like a normal person? She picks up the box and gives it a shake as if panning for gold. The trinkets and left behinds rattle a little and sift apart. Then she sees it. The journal. Words and drawings. Someone else's thoughts and emotions. Emily pulls the journal out and sets it on the counter. She stares at it. Whether hastily written or thoroughly planned out, this book is private. Yet she feels like she is under a spell, that something is pulling her hand closer and closer. Like a little devil on her shoulder, the whisper comes, enticing her to evil. Emily bites her lip. She shrugs off any pangs of guilt or fear. Without another thought or hesitation she tosses the journal into her backpack.

Dom shows up like clockwork and walks her home. He tries to tell her jokes and tease her, but she's lost in her own mind. What had she done? Did she really have that thing in her bag?

"Hey, you okay? Dom asks. You seem a little out of it."

No it's not alright, it's all wrong. She's so involved in her guilt trip she doesn't remember if she answers Dom. Maybe she mumbled a "Yeah I'm fine," or maybe she just shrugged her shoulders. Soon she finds herself at her door. Dom stands back as per tradition and begins to bid her farewell and goodnight. She forgets to thank him for being a weird chivalrous kind of guy, and shuts the door before he can finish.

Sitting crisscross on her bed, Emily has the book laid out in her lap, looking her in the face. The pages seem to question her motives. The room is dark, with only the dim bedside lamp lit.

Hiding from something? Emily runs her fingers over the journal, still not sure what her own intentions are. With lip bit and another sting of guilt she opens the cover.

"This Book Belongs To: blank. Come on, Blue Girl. How about a clue?" Emily says. Then realizes she's said it out loud. Was she talking to the book now? Oh goodness. The tension fills the small room. Almost willing to stop, Emily compulsively turns the page. The first entry is dated nearly a year ago. It starts with the normal This-is-my-life kind of entry. Blue Girl was a thirty-something with a rough past but decent outlook. She lived in the city and worked an eight to five. She had recently found a new love and regained partial custody of her four year old daughter. She was cleaning up and flying straight. She sounded so happy.

"Stuff is finally going right," Blue Girl wrote. "I have my little girl on the weekends and a true love every day. He's helping me keep clean and be a better person." Smiley faces, hearts and funny birds decorate the margins. Emily smiles. Several entries follow. Things building to a progression of a better life. Blue Girl and Prince Wonderful along with the little girl all living happily ever...but wait. Something worrying begins to color the text. A heavy mood that leaves Emily with a knot in her stomach. A few entries later, it happens. The very thing Emily didn't want to read.

"It's all gone to hell again. I guess happy endings were never meant for me." it starts. Emily physically sinks. The familiarity of it, the expectation of what was going to happen next. Like a snow globe falling from a top shelf, though it seems to plummet in slow motion you are also caught in the time warp and completely unable to catch or save it. You know for what seems an eternity that it will crash and it will shatter. Shards will be scattered across the floor and the little figures who were once safe inside will be exposed and likely broken. Emily doesn't want to know this about someone else; she doesn't like knowing it about herself. Once you've been washed out to sea, you have only to swim on, so Emily reads more. Prince Wonderful faltered. Or maybe Blue Girl did, but the Prince bore the fault of the failing. He was untrue, he was needy and ungiving. He didn't listen and always argued. The stress was piling up on Blue Girl and everything else was becoming discolored and distasteful. Her straight flight had been knocked off kilter. She had taken some bad turns and was in danger of losing her daughter again. Emily feels a shiver at some remembrance of her own failings. Stuck with a dangerous man she thought she loved. Facing her own demons in the toilet bowl while barfing in a motel room you rent by the hour. Emily takes a deep cleansing breath, wanting so badly to forget. With trembling hands she closes the journal. How long had she been reading? It had only felt like moments, but now she felt tired and beaten and knew it must have been at least an hour. Oh, make that two. The realization is disquieting as she notices the clock. Nearly midnight, she has experienced months of another's life in a matter of one hundred and twenty minutes. Another cleansing breath and she closes her eyes to vanish into troubled sleep.

Chapter 4 – Loose Wires

SHAKEN BY her late night reading, Emily struggles to start her day with the normal energy and enthusiasm. The crisis in the book is jarringly familiar, so many pieces slipping on a decidedly downward slide to something haunting and inevitable. She forces herself to remember that the written events happened months ago and may no longer represent Blue Girl's current condition. And familiar as they seem, Emily's own path has transformed into something smooth and perhaps even promising. So on she dances, drawing up the energy and courage to face a new day with vigor and vision. Over the months she has been in this small town making a life and working in the roadhouse, she has found an inner music. An inner music filled with melodies of optimism and confidence. Maybe not the peace that she had initially hoped for, but perhaps more harmonies will join in later. The music is strong and growing ever stronger; she is becoming content. What was once a place for hiding in the shadows of inconspicuousness, now is becoming a place to blossom and shine in the sun.

For the first time in years she is beginning to feel free. The journal, and Blue Girl are showing her just how far she has come, by reminding her of where she started. So now, from table to table pouring coffee, picking up plates, mopping up after kids, she moves with ease. It is all hard work but she soaks up all the smiles and relishes bringing them to her customers. Sloughing off the fetters of her past, she twirls and skips as her soiled apron flares out like a skirt. Every day is the same crowd, but with different faces. For only moments each day they are in her life. A fifteen minute cup of joe, a thirty minute meal, a last minute bathroom stop. It was a funny sort of life she had stumbled upon, but a place she could make herself happy. So on she dances, energy building, optimism singing. Ready to make the day new.

Harry and Caroline watch her move around. Caroline shakes her head at what she obviously sees as some strange spectacle.

"She'll wear herself out, moving like that," she scoffs. Harry bumps her disapprovingly.

"Agh, let her dance. In fact, I think you should dance around like that. The people seem to like it and they may even leave bigger tips." Caroline rolls her eyes, refusing to respond. Harry smiles and leans in closely to her.

"I'd sure tip ya good."

"Is that so? Well in that case." She smiles grandly and wafts her hands around his face then mockingly dances away. Her hips sashay and feet glide as she moves down the hall. Harry wolf whistles at her. Without turning or looking she waves him away and disappears into the office.

~~~~~~~~~~

The bell on the door jingles slightly, then clatters to the floor. It sadly sits on the floor between the toes of two well worn work boots. A middle aged truckdriver stands stunned staring at the bell by his feet. His tall frame and broad shoulders seems to fill the whole doorway.

"Uhh, sorry," he mutters sheepishly as if he'd done something malicious to knock the bell from its place. Emily hurries over, snaps it up and looks it over.

"Is it hurt badly?" the trucker asks. Emily looks up from the quandary of the trinket. Her expression melts into chagrin for ignoring her customer.

"Oh, I'm sorry, sir. --"

"Not 'Sir', no call me Buck. That's what it says on my shirt." Sure enough his shirt proclaims his name to be Buck.

"Is that your name?" Emily inquires. The Trucker smiles.

"No, but that's what my shirt says." Emily laughs and motions to the open dining room. She welcomes him in and invites him to sit with a promise of hot coffee. Buck smiles and happily finds a place.

"So will it live?" Buck asks as Emily pours his coffee. A moment of complete loss crosses her face until she remembers the bell. She retrieves it from her pocket.

"Yeah, it's okay, just a loose wire." She shakes the bell and shows him the unraveled wire that is supposed to hold the bell in place.

"I understand that." Buck smiles. "Got a few loose wires myself," he says with a slight wink.

"Someone is supposed to bring me some things to fix it, but I'll have to juryrig it until he brings them," Emily says with a sigh.

"Nothing wrong with making do," Buck affirms and takes a sip of his coffee.

Emily smiles. She quickly takes Buck's order and delivers it to Harry. When she again has a free moment the young waitress quickly picks up a chair, sets it by the door and climbs up. How often has she stood on this chair this week? Goodness. She spends a few moments fidgeting and fiddling with the wire, trying to get it to hold the bell securely. Finally assured of her success, again, she takes her hands away and puts the chair back. She looks at the bell and smiles, but doubt crosses her mind. This isn't going to last. Gradually she turns but the bell soon calls her back as it announces another entrant. As if on cue Dom has come with a paper sack in hand. He holds up the bag to show Emily. She feels a smile cross her face and motions for him to join her at the side counter. With a quick nod he follows her over.

Emily feels an odd excitement to see what goodies he's brought her. Dom sets the bag down and slowly opens it.

"Now," he says hesitantly. "Don't hate me for this."

Emily scowls. What did he do? Dom pulls a brand new bell and hanger attachment from the sack. Emily instantly shakes her head vehemently no.

"Absolutely not," she says, not willing to give an inch.

"Oh come now, let's keep the options open here. It might--" he starts but is quickly cut off.

"No. I'm not going to just throw it away because it's not gonna be easy to fix."

"Okay, I hear you," Dom says as he looks down, shoulders sinking. "I suspected that might be your stance, so I did bring--" He cuts himself off and dumps out the rest of the contents. Before them now is a spread of various hardware bits; from wire and tools to a roll of polka dotted duct tape. Polka dot duct tape?

"Really?" Emily asks holding up the tape. Dom smiles mischievously and tells her that he figured the gray color would just be too boring for her. What do you know, he's right. Emily makes a face. Mr. Nineteen-Forties has some insights. Emily thanks him and starts to clear the counter of the all the hardware bits.

"So, I can help you, if you want," he offers with quiet hope, and puppy dog eyes. A moment to think and Emily slowly shakes her head and tells him thank you but no. She realizes that she really wants to fix it herself. The desire is strange. She's never been handy or the fix-it type, and now she's fighting for the chance to be just that.

"Alrighty then," Dom says with final resignation, though he seems to be hesitant to say it. He does a little drumming on the counter and starts to move to the door. "I'll see you tonight?"

"I'll be here," she answers. He grins again. Cute, charming and sweet, almost too perfect. Stop it! He is too perfect, she would wreck him. Emily groans to herself and tries to put it aside. As Dom vanishes out the door, she has to shake herself out of watching him go. No, she won't get involved. He doesn't need her baggage.

Once the counter is cleared, Emily also clears her mind. She takes off again agilely moving around the roadhouse, gradually building momentum as she gathers dishes in a big gray tub and dances to the kitchen. Caroline mans the counter when a frazzled businessman comes in the door. He plasters a map on the countertop.

"I need help," he says blatantly.

"I'm sure you do," Caroline says, looking him over. "Emily, someone needs your help," she calls out and walks away.

"Caroline, why don't you.... never mind." Emily comes over and asks the man what she can do for him.

"I'm lost. I'm so very, extremely lost," he says then motions his hands over the map. "I don't even know where I am. What town is this? Is this a town? Or just some glorified rest area without a name? I don't even know how I got here. I swear the road just dumped me here. I was just following my GPS and then I was... here. Mini Hell with strange waitresses."

Emily's eyebrows shoot up. Her expression goes from shock to fury to forced calm. "Why don't you show me where you're trying to go, and maybe I can help." Emily speaks deliberately, mustering all the calm that she can, though she can feel this guy plucking on her last nerve already. He looks to her and is about to speak when he stops short.

"Hello?" he says louder than necessary. "Yes, I know! I'm completely lost in Mini Hell right now." He goes on talking and retelling most of what he's already said. Emily is confused until she realizes he's on the phone. He puts his hand on the little earpiece stuck to the side of his head.

"What? I know, the reception is terrible. I know, it's a disaster, try to keep 'em happy for another hour, right? Yeah. Right, whatever." Emily watches him pace as he talks. She catches glances from a few of the diners in the room. This Psycho Man is starting to unsettle people. Abruptly he turns to her again. She stands shocked by the quick maneuver. He motions her to the map. She starts to ask again where he's trying to go. But he doesn't hear her.

"No! Don't do that!" He turns away and shouts and motions with his hands. Emily jumps back a little and scowls. "No, whatever you do.... yeah, that's what I'm saying." Psycho Man comes back and points to the map. She looks at the location, studying the predicament. She hums to herself as she tries to figure out the directions. The sooner she can get this guy out of here the better. She looks up to find him inches from her face. Emily's insides jump at the surprise. Snap. There it goes. That was her last nerve.

"Hmm?" he asks, exasperated. "Don't tell me I can't get there from here."

"Well..." she hesitates, still trying to figure it out.

"Ha!" he shouts, throwing his hands up again and walking in a full circle. Emily shrinks a little. She wonders if there's a separate emergency number for insane people. Why did Caroline have to dump this bozo on her? Because she's clever, that's why.

"It's okay, I think--" she starts to say.

"Okay? Is it really? How can it possibly be okay?" With more exaggerated arm throwing and exasperated shouting, he continues to exclaim. "My career is hanging in the balance here. If I don't show up in an hour the biggest deal of my life slips through my fingers. But it's okay, because Waitress Oh-So-Helpful says it's going to be 'okay!'"

That's it. "Hey!" she shouts as she slams her hands down on the counter. The dining room full of people who have been trying to avoid this conversation are now completely captivated by it. The realization that she has an audience gives her pause, but she muscles through it for the sake of that very audience.

"Enough already! Chill the freak out or I will have someone escort you to your car and you can find your own freaking way!" Silence. Tense, horrible silence. Psycho Man glances around finally aware of the attention he's garnered. Emily shudders as the adrenaline and fury drain a little. Yet there is still a hint of rage hardening her eyes. She takes a deep breath and points back to his map. Her sweet genuine tone shakily recovers as she begins to explain how he can make his way to his destination. She writes down the turn by turn directions, makes him a coffee to go, and invites him to leave. He takes a deep breath like he's about to make another comment when a large shadow drifts over him. Buck and one of his buddies stand over Psycho Man.

"I believe," Buck says in a tone slower and deeper than his standard timbre, "the young lady has given you more than enough help." Psycho Man shrinks about two inches, grabs his coffee, murmurs some dubious form of thanks and slinks out the door.

As the door closes the bell falls again. Emily makes a face. Psycho Man broke my bell. The strange desire to chase him down and pelt him with the bell comes over her but quickly fades. It'd probably do more damage to the poor trinket, already sorely abused. Buck goes over and picks up the bell and looks it over.

"I'm afraid it's more than loose wires this time," he comments and hands it to Emily. This time a piece is actually broken, not just bent or misshapen. There seems to be no way to hang it again. Perplexed, Emily takes a seat on one of the barstools and slowly swings back and forth. The stool squeaks slightly with her movements. It was only a matter of time until she wouldn't be able to fix it again, but she isn't about to let this be the final word. This loyal little noisemaker has been a part of the diner for years now, decades perhaps. Enough moping. She stuffs the bell in her apron pocket and hops to her feet. She'll find a moment to examine more closely the problem and any possible solutions. For the next few hours she rings and clatters with every step and flourish. Many giggles and smiles follow the jingling waitress as she makes her rounds. She enjoys the accompaniment for a while and thinks maybe she should always keep a bell in her pocket. However, as is often the case, the newness of the unique predicament begins to wear and grow tired after a while. Now the sound is grating with every jingle-jangle step.

Finally a break in the rush comes and she escapes to the back to once again look into the problem of the bell. Yep, it's still broken. The happy time in her pocket did not miraculously cure its ills. Emily grabs the bag of hardware goodies that Dom brought her. She rummages through to find various wire, snips, string, some hooks and other hanging hardware, all of which were now completely useless. In the bottom of the sack she finds it. The holy grail that could possibly fix her problem. Duct tape. Polka dot duct tape. Without another thought she rips a piece of tape off and begins to fold and stick and configure it into something that will hold the bell in place but not hinder its sound. She carries the newly created Franken-Bell out to the door. Caroline catches a glimpse of her.

"Oh no. It's been so quiet in here without that thing ringing, can't you just leave it off?" Caroline whines.

"Absolutely not," Emily stoutly shakes her head. How can she even ask such a thing? The little trinket is a fixture in the roadhouse, it's required hardware for a diner door. There has to be a bell!

Caroline looks again, now noticing the polka dots. "What have you done to it?"

Emily smiles and skips a step. "I fixed it," she says proudly, standing a bit taller. Caroline only rolls her eyes. Emily pulls up the chair and goes to rehanging the bell. After a moment of fussing and meddling and a few more pieces of tape the bell is hung. Emily steps down and gently tests the door. The bell chimes with less jingle and more muffled clanking, but it is still a cheerful noise. Emily smiles proudly. Harry, who has been covertly watching and eavesdropping chuckles and calls out.

"Well done!"

"Don't encourage her, Harry," Caroline snaps. She points a finger at Emily. "You won't be able to fix it many more times." Emily only smiles. There's still a whole roll of duct tape.

~~~~~~~~~

The roadhouse is all but empty, with only a few single road warriors scattered inside, and for the moment all are content. With a hot coffee mounded with whipped topping, Emily carefully makes her way to the back booth. The very booth that, days ago, the Blue Girl had taken her respite. She sits quietly, gazing out the window, warming her hands on the steaming mug. The sky is stricken pink as the sun slowly sets, the clouds glow golden and still the cars roll by. The waitress wonders how many of those wayfarers were savoring the sky and how many couldn't see past the miles and miles of road ahead of them. How many are so focused on the pavement that they won't see the scenery, let alone stop and enjoy it. She takes a sip of her coffee and a quick glance around before she pulls out the journal. What is happening to her? Why did she bring it with her? If Caroline caught her with it, oh, the questions that would follow. She would be subjected to interrogation and quite possibly torture. Harry, however, would be far worse if he caught her. He would want to talk to her about it. Not in a condemning way, no he'd wanna know why and want to talk about her feelings. The prospect is more frightening than Caroline's torture. Besides, she doesn't know what she is feeling or why she is so drawn into the book. It isn't mere curiosity. It's something more, something begging her to read it and get something more from it. So, carefully, stealthily and guiltily Emily cracks open the pages. She carefully slides out the ribbon bookmark, ready to use cat-like reflexes to close and stow the book if need be. Gradually the diner melts away as she again immerses herself in someone else's life.

"I'm completely trapped," Blue Girl wrote. Months had past since Prince Wonderful suffered a fall from grace. Piece by piece the rest of her life was coming apart as well. All her goals and determination seemed to work against her and she only grew more isolated, distracted, and misaimed. And then, in the next entry the tone changed. The writer changed. Blue Girl was packing her bags and leaving. "There's no hope for change, unless I make it myself." Leaving the old life behind and seeking out something new. That sounds familiar. It takes Emily back to her decision. To stay, and remain oppressed and stuck. Or to escape, venture out on her own. It was terrifying, but liberating. She still wakes up frightened though, worrying that maybe something from her old life has found her.

A bell rings. Emily feels her insides jump. With less than a ninja reaction she clumsily replaces the ribbon, closes the book and jams it back into her pack. She jumps up and grabs her coffee mug. It's empty. When had she finished it? A quick glance out the window reveals that it is now twilight; the colors have shifted to the deep velvet blue of evening. She looks to the door. No one has come or gone. A bell rings again. A traveler stands by the cash register and rings the bell on the counter. With the realization Emily hurriedly apologizes and makes her way to take care of the check.

Chapter 5 – Lids Are Overrated

LYING IN BED Emily knows she should go to sleep. Lights out. It's already after midnight; she has another twelve hour shift to hit in the morning. And yet the book, that stupid book, is calling her again. This new obsession is becoming exhausting. With a groan she sits up, not willing to fight it anymore. She turns on the light, fishes the journal from her backpack and snuggles back into bed to read. Just a few pages, then she'll turn the light out. No problem.

"It's all behind me. Tethers cut, possessions sold. There is nothing to keep me there any more," Blue Girl started her entry. She was headed for the coast to meet an old flame. The Knight in Shining Armor that she thought Prince Wonderful could replace. But the truth was obvious now, he was the only one she could ever love. Selling everything had afforded her less than four hundred dollars and left her wondering how far she could actually get. A friend had given her a car; it smelled like old french fries and she was pretty sure something had died in the air conditioner. After only one full day on the road, and an eerie night at a rest stop, the car sputtered once and quickly succumbed. All life left the vehicle and was spirited away along with the eighty mile an hour traffic. Undeterred, she started to walk, leaving most of her remaining belongings in the car. With only a backpack full of essentials and precious things across her shoulders she started walking. Walking and catching rides when she could. Sun and rain beat down on Blue Girl; resolute in her mind, she willfully marched on.

Emily closes the book, unable to keep her eyes open any longer. The clock reads sometime after two A.M., but her vision is too blurry to make it all out. With a groan she buries the book under her pillow. Work is gonna suck in the morning.

Come daylight Emily shuts off the alarm with terrifying vengeance and forces herself out of bed. She arrives at the roadhouse not quite at her peak performance. Caroline's eyes follow her in and over to the coffee pots. The caffeine is calling to her. Still feeling Caroline's gaze Emily feels her muscles tighten.

"Good morning, Caroline," she says, her voice barely audible. Caroline beams. Oh, she's loving this.

"Emily, honey. Did you forget to go to bed last night?" Caroline inquires. Emily takes a slow methodical drink of the fresh brew, taking her sweet time calculating her answer.

"Stayed up too long--" Emily pauses, contemplating, "Reading," she admits finally. Inside she cringes and wills Caroline not to ask about her choice of reading material. Caroline nods and moves on with her morning chores. Phew! For the rest for the morning Emily forces herself to keep moving as every time she stops her eyes try to close and her body cries out for sleep.

With every covered yawn and creak of her tired bones she begs to herself to stop thinking about the journal. Yet she feels it is all leading to something. Something important. Blue Girl's life unfolding before her is strikingly irresistible. The familiarity and resemblance to her own life, being stuck in a horrible relationship and taking strides to be free of it.

The day progresses, as only the really annoying days can. The fatigue leads to distraction, leads to uncoordinated actions, leads to messes. By noon, Emily has been bathed in spilled soup, smeared in cherry pie, and exploded on by the blender. Her clothes have gone from wet and sticky to dry and crusty. Flustered by the last straw she throws herself down on a stool by the bar.

"What else could possibly go wrong today?" She instantly regrets saying it.

"Oh, you did not just say that, did you?" Caroline demands as she shoots her a glare. Emily bites her lip and sheepishly nods. "Oh, honey," Caroline chides, but is interrupted by the muffled Franken-Bell, a sound that earns Emily another scolding look. She shrinks away and goes to greet the new customers. With some effort she finds a rhythm and skips her way over to the tables. She scribbles down some orders and points a few rather desperate looking people in the direction of the restrooms. Once they are settled she again plops down on a barstool. Slowly she rubs her face, stretches her shoulders and rolls her head back and forth, when out of the corner of her eye something catches her attention. She looks up to see a nervous man walking out from the back where the bathrooms are. Something is strange in the way he leaves. Like he's trying not to run, but wants desperately to get away. Oh no. Emily catches his eye.

"Is everything ok, sir? Are you alright?" she asks. The man hesitates and tries to stop but keeps rocking and edging toward the door.

"Uh," he starts then looks away toward the door. "There's... uh... something... wrongwiththebathroom!" he finally blurts out then hurries out the door. Caroline sees what has transpired and looks at Emily with real fear in her eyes.

"Run." It's a command; firm and urgent. The strange look of panic on Caroline's face is enough to make Emily race down the hall toward the bathroom. A moment passes.

"Ahhhhh!" comes a holler. Emily has reached her destination. Caroline looks toward the kitchen. "Harry, get the mop bucket!"

In the bathroom, more screaming ensues as Emily stands in the doorway, the toilet spewing water in heaps and rushes. It streams across the floor in an ever mounting flood. Emily shrieks and groans as she finally gets the nerve to step into the breach. The water seeps into her shoes. It's cold and nasty and horrible. She groans deeply. The toilet keeps cycling and filling and overflowing in an appalling pattern of watery disaster.

"I hate my job!" she growls as she tries flipping the handle up and down. No change. She grabs the plunger and jam, jam, jams it in and out. Nothing helps.

"AHHHH!!" The water continues to splash down at her feet

and gets soaked up by her pant legs. Everything she tries fails. She screams with anger every few moments just to convey how absolutely awful it is. With a final shout of dismay she slams the seat and lid down with a crash. Spitefully the water continues to seep out from under the lid. Once again lids have failed her. Finally she notices the shut off valve on the pipe on the floor and reaches into the water to turn it off. The toilet stops cycling, finally. But the water continues to trickle down the bowl. Gradually it tapers off and stops. The adrenaline finally levels out and Emily realizes she's still standing in a flood.

"Caroline!" she cries. A pause, silence. Did they abandon her? Is she completely alone? "Harry?" She begs for a reply, "I need help." Her pitiful cry is met with Harry sloshing in wearing tall muck boots. Emily is incredulous. "Where were those?" Harry smiles apologetically as he hands her the mop and bucket. Emily tries not to glare as she takes them from him and he slowly turns and leaves her there. She looks around apathetically and gradually takes in the full scale fiasco in front of her. She wants to cry, or laugh, or scream... again... but she can't decide which. So she sets the bucket down and throws the mop into the flood and begins to sop up the freakish disaster.

~~~~~~~~~~

"Vile, monstrous piece of-- argh!" Emily curses the appliance again while sitting at the bar, shoes still squishy, pants wet nearly up to her knees. Caroline brings her a mug of coffee with whipped cream.

"It's a toilet, Em," she states.

Emily vehemently disagrees . "It's evil! Spiteful, vengeful..." she trails off with a grunt and sticks out her lower lip. A pouty face that would rival even the saddest three year old. So many wonderful words and yet they all fail to describe how violated she feels at the moment. She gives up and takes a sip of the hot drink. Then looking down at her clothes she makes a face.

"Can I go home? Please? I wanna go change... and never come back." She laughs at herself, though she really doesn't find it funny.

"Yes, by all means. Go get clean. But I'm afraid you do have to come back," Caroline says nodding.

Fair enough.

Emily slumps into the motel room. Oh, the bed looks nice and inviting, but she wouldn't dare put her murky self in those nice clean sheets. Heaving a sigh she mopes her way through turning on the shower. She looks herself over, and contemplates throwing her clothes in the trash rather than trying to wash this day out of them. Ugh.

Once clean and refreshed, Emily is dressed and ready to venture back out. But first, she sees the journal. Oops, that was a mistake. Caroline didn't say when she had to be back. She could probably read another entry or two and not be missed... too much. Besides, she had earned it. Right?

Blue Girl continued her brave walkabout to the coast. Days of travel and she was getting close. She had met some great people on the road and her spirits were high. But something changes. There's a gap in the entries. A page has been ripped out and the next few pages have angry scribbles and hateful words on them. Halfway down the installment starts.

"He won't return my calls. He said it was complicated and might not work out. Now nothing." Blue Girl's Knight had tarnished armor. Her rose colored glasses had fallen to the floor and she was finally seeing clearly. She realized she was on a fool's errand and needed to become grounded again. Broken hearted Blue Girl was more lost than she had ever been before. The next page, stained with dry tears, was dated two days later. Blue Girl found herself in a little roadhouse called Vinny's in a little hole in the road town. The waitress seemed nice. A portion of the entry was scratched out then she continued.

"They're taking her away from me." The father of her little girl was calling her unfit and taking away all visitation rights. Blue Girl tried to call her daughter, but the little girl was too frightened to talk to her mother. It was her last chance, and it slipped through her fingers. No one wanted her. No one needed her. She had become a burden and a nuisance. The entry ends abruptly. The next page is different; unlike those that came before, this one bears only a single sentence. The words send ice down Emily's veins. Chills rush through her limbs and bring her to a frozen halt, her hands clammy, her lips quivering. A tear slips down her face. She's reached the Blue Girl's last written page. Wait. Had she read that right?

"There's a bridge I know of... and I should be gone forever." More thoughts and ideas rush into Emily's mind than she can handle. Did Blue Girl really mean it? Had she left the journal on purpose as a final message? Was someone else supposed to read it? Her daughter, maybe? Oh, that poor little girl. Emily's stomach churns with agony. She wraps her arms around herself and rocks and weeps. Tears stream down her face; she closes her eyes in an effort to stop them. But as the pattern has proven, closing lids does nothing. Cruelly the tears continue to seep through. Emily longs for the words on the page to change, but they don't. Anger wells up in her; it floods in and fills her with a strong desire to rip out this last horrible page, slam the journal closed and throw it across the room with a scream. But instead she closes it firmly as her hands grip the book tightly, strangling the binding. How dare she just give up, and leave her poor little girl at home. Things can be terrible, but still there can be hope. Dammit! The tears keep coming.

A gentle knock comes on the door.

"Em? You home?" Harry's voice calls quietly from the other side. Crap, what's he doing here? Emily wants so badly to be alone in her misery. That's how it's always been.

"Em?" Harry calls again with another quiet knock. Emily rolls her eyes upward. The tears aren't going to stop for the asking. Can't hide forever, besides Harry's likely to knock the door down if he's really worried about her.

"Yeah," she squeaks. "I'm here."

"You okay?" he asks, filled with concern. Emily stands and unlocks the door. Face to face with the big man in her doorway, her eyes fill all over again.

"Hey." Instant worry fills his voice as he steps in and puts his hands on her shoulders. "What's going on?" With a sob Emily falls against Harry and weeps into his shoulder. He slowly wraps his arms around her, embracing her in the warmest, safest bear hug she's ever felt. Emily can't make herself pull away. He feels so safe, she doesn't ever want to leave his grasp. After a long moment of silent sobs Emily pulls away and shows him the journal still clutched in her hand. They sit on the bed and she tells him about the Blue Girl and her obsessive reading. Then the last entry. The disclosure turns to Emily's own story. She spares him details but shares how the Blue Girl could easily be a mirror of herself. Harry takes it all in stride, patiently, quietly listening without judgment. The confession is painful, yet cleansing, like dumping out a bucket of water. The fluid pulls against the bucket until it's empty and then it feels so extremely light. The burden is gone. The tears dry. Emily is more exhausted than she's ever been before, but she's never felt so free.

"So, what do I do with this?" she asks, holding up the book. Harry looks her firmly in the eyes and takes the book from her hand.

"Don't let this be you."

~~~~~~~~~~

Emily stands on a chair hanging the bell. The new bell. She

finishes and slowly takes her hands away. The new brass chime glimmers in the morning sun. It looks solid and secure. Dom picked a good one. She taps it, the ring like a shimmer of sound crisp and pure. It echoes through the room. Emily thwacks the bell a few more times, making it ring out in cheerful protest. She smiles to herself with satisfaction. The little bell seems very content to hold strong and jingle happily.

"Enough already!" Caroline calls. "My ears are ringing."

Emily springs down off the chair as Caroline and Harry come out with a small package wrapped in newspaper.

"Are you ready to go?" Harry asks in such a gentle and quiet tone that Emily suspects perhaps he's fighting back tears. Emily feels her eyes well up as she nods affirmation.

Caroline rolls her eyes. "No, no. No crying! Quick, give it to her before we all start bawling." Harry snuffles a little and hands Emily the package. She reluctantly accepts the gift and begins to unwrap it.

"You guys really shouldn't have. I'm only gonna be gone a few weeks and then I'm coming right--" The paper falls away. Emily laughs and holds up a t-shirt with "Carpe Diem" printed on it. She laughs again and then starts to cry again. Caroline goes to her and embraces her tightly. More tightly than expected. Twelve short months ago Caroline and Harry were strangers, but she feels now like she's known them forever.

The bell rings, a chipper little sound. Emily finds herself expecting the sound to be followed by a clattering sound on the floor, but this bell doesn't fall off. Dom comes in, and looks up at the bell, noticing the new sound. He looks at Emily with shock; she gives him a coy little wink and a shrug.

"Car's here." Dom says casually. "It's not pretty, and kinda smells like my high school locker, but she's reliable." He hands Emily some keys; all of a sudden she's a lot more hesitant to accept them. But as she reaches for them, Dom catches her hand and kisses it. Emily feels her face glowing and can't keep herself from smiling. Mr. Nineteen-Forties strikes again. Stop it!

Dom holds the door open, smiling sweetly at her. With a deep breath of determination and resolve Emily steps out the door. Reaching in her pocket, she pulls the old bell out. The old broken bauble tinkles a little in her hand. With her friendly polka dotted duct tape she fastens the bell to the rear view mirror of the car.

After a final round of goodbyes, she sets off. Harry, Caroline and Dom are standing in front of Vinny's Roadhouse waving fond farewells and bon voyage. What a strange little family she's found in this funny hole in the road town. It started as a hiding place, but then she found herself. Now is the time to make amends for her past, do some exploring and then she'll come back. Back home.

The End?

"Freedom" by Ellie Christina

I sat on the chilled floor of the heartless dungeon awaiting my death sentence. My mind became immersed in the memories of my corruption; the same corruption that defiled a thousand years of ancestors before me. An inescapable fate that had chased me down since the day I was born. I was proud to be a part of such a long standing heritage, yet in anguish at the coming end.

The thick wooden cell door opened. Anxiety grew in my heart. A blinding light of hope bathed me in surprising brilliance. Freedom was at the gate; his intense spirit beckoned me. Humanly, I doubted his authenticity and was reluctant to leave the deadly home I'd known for so long. Freedom called to me again. Hesitantly I stood to answer. Finding more courage, I ran from my prison cell and agilely ascended the stairs. Seeing a guard, I slowed and carefully slipped past. I was unstoppable. Moving swiftly through the courtyard, I scrambled over the surrounding stone wall to find a dense forest waiting for me. I charged through the thick brush, dodging trees and rocks. Finally I burst into a clearing.

A beautiful pasture lay before me, so I rested. A proud spirit came over me, for I had escaped the inescapable. The grass radiated blue under the moonlight and intensified the sense of the empty expanse. Gray clouds began to creep in and a heavy fog pulled itself sluggishly across the field. Hope disappeared conjointly with the moonlight as all became dark. Freedom had left me. Abandoned, I crouched down in dread like a wilting flower fearful of the coming winter. The awe of my amazing escape vanished completely when I heard the sound of the approaching guards. I gazed into the vast meadow wondering how to disappear.

My eye scoured the area for safety. Should I run for the trees or seek shelter in the mountains? As the guards grew nearer, I doubted if either would be a safe haven. I wondered if there would be any escape in this last and desperate attempt to survive.

I felt a shadow drift over me. Fear gripped my soul; I shuddered with an eerie expectation. Turning my gaze upward I saw Freedom standing above me. I followed his gaze to the now visible battalion of approaching guards. Without a word exchanged I knew the thoughts that burdened Freedom's mind. Self-denial and sacrifice filled the air. Questions filled my mind. Disbelief froze my reactions. Before I could object, the guards were upon us. Brutally they beat the innocent one while I, the guilty, lay in bittersweet safety. All became quiet; I thought Freedom must be dead.

The sun was cresting the evergreen mountains, beautifully blanketed in a satiny mist while they lay their heads on a pillow of clouds. The long grass of the field waved in the gentle breeze like the softest fur being stroked by an invisible hand. The serenity was surreal.

Suddenly a warm wind swept up around me. Instinct led me deep into the forest. Coming to a splintery cross, I stopped when something caught my eye. Broken bonds lay at the foot of the cross. I felt warmth and comfort for the first time. Freedom now stood in front of me alive and smiling. He told me that Freedom cannot be killed, that he will always exist even if just in your heart.

The End?

TABLE OF CONTENTS

Chapter 7
The Visitors

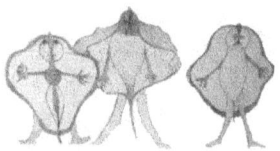

Hours later in the alley, three fish-looking aliens appeared with a special kind of scanner that showed flashes of green light where Time and Flip transported. The device that aliens have help them see where the crust has been used.

The aliens transport back to their planet called, Mackton. It is a water planet five times the size of the earth, with four moons surrounding it. Only one section of the planet, about the size of our moon, still contains water. The rest of the planet is dry and dusty with no life. The aliens that live there are a very sophisticated race called, Macktonians. There are about 100 thousand of them left on their planet. At one time there were several million of them. They are a peaceful race. There has never been war in their history. Of the three aliens that came to earth, two were brothers and the third one, the king, is their father.

Many years earlier there was a storm that hit their city, washing away most of the palace. The pebble is how they use most of their technology. The pebble was in the palace when it was washed away. It was lost for months. The aliens travelled to the dry parts of their planet to find it. One day they saw a spaceship where their scanners said the pebble was. In fear, not ever seeing a spaceship before, or humans they stayed hidden. As the spaceship left the signal disappeared.

Knowing they took the pebble. After searching the galaxy for over 20 years, they found that it had been used on Earth.

Arriving back to the kingdom, the older brother was not happy with his father. They have a human captured in a special device to keep him alive. It is a glass tube filled with oxygen. The older son is upset because this human could tell his people how to save the planet but at this time the human will not talk.

The aliens know that he knows where the pebble is because they used the device to see were the crust had been used. It showed green signals all over the area where they had captured him. The older brother says, "We can make this human talk." The king says to his older son, "We are a peaceful race. Yes, we might have means to make him talk, but it's not right. I would send him back to his own planet if not for what he might tell them about us and cause war." "Yes, Father, I know, but if he doesn't tell us about earth and where that pebble is, we will all be lost and our planet will be no more! He knows where that pebble is. The humans took it from our planet and this one knows something. The scanners showed green light all over him. It is only fair for us to get it back by any means, so we all may live." The younger brother was standing to the side starting to say something, but the older brother motioned for him to be quiet. The younger brother was small and skinny and not brave enough to question his brother. As the father and sons' argument continued to get more heated the younger brother stepped farther into the corner. The older brother said, "King, you just let your people die." Stepping towards the king. "Son this is best for the kingdom, stand down!" the brother continues to get closer to the King, and grabs him as he walks away. "If you do not allow me to get the information from that human, I will tell your people that you are going to let them die for a human". The king walks towards him and pushes him to the ground, "I am doing it to save the kingdom". The older brother, in anger, stands up and runs toward the king and knocks him to the ground. He stabs him with his tail saying, "If you can't save our people, I will". He stabbed him right in the heart. The other brother watched in fear saying, "What did you do?" "I just saved our planet" said the older brother, Lucas. He and his father have been fighting for years about the condition of their planet and on this day, he just could not take anymore and killed the king. His younger brother did not dare to question him. His hate for his father and his willingness to do anything to save his people, no matter what, made him dangerous. Most of the kingdom feared him. He told the guards, "The king is dead, and I am the new king. Go get the electric eels. We will put them on that human. I am going to save this planet."

The new king walked into the room where they had the human. "Guards, open it up and put the eel on him". The guards opened the class tube where the human is. Water rushes in, they put a mask on the human so he can breathe. They connected the eel to his spine and resealed the enclosure. Then they drain the water out. King Lucas holds in his hand, a controller that causes the eels start to electrocute the human. The king says in an angry voice, "TELL ME ABOUT

EARTH AND WHERE THAT
PEBBLE IS!"

Chapter 8
Game Changer

Two weeks have passed since Time and Flips encounter with Scarlet. Time is in the basement of his garage listening to scanners and the TV for any reports of emergencies, as he was busy working on computers and new devices. Flip comes sliding down the ladder. Saying, "Calm before the storm". Time raised his head and said, "What? Flip answered, "Still nothing going on yet? It has been a quiet two weeks." "No, nothing." Time said. "What storm are you talking about? The storm that's coming?" "No, just something my grandmother used to say." "Oh." Time said laughing. Flip says, "It just means it's calm now then it's going to get busy. What have you been working on?"

"Not a lot, just some defense weapons in case we encounter someone like Scarlet again." "Cool." Flip said. "What are you doing with one of my old skateboards?" Time grabs it." Look," he says, "it breaks in half where you can block strikes from something like a sword or another weapon. It goes on your arms." "Cool, I like that." "Your watch looks new. Does that do something cool?" Flip asked. "Yes." Time said. "It shoots out a small cable and whatever the end of

it is touching I can send that object back in time anywhere I want to."
"Wow! that is so cool!" Flips says. He grabs his new skateboard and stands on it. He tries to flip it up into the air onto his arms and misses and knocks over a lamp, breaking it. "Oops!" Flip said, "I guess I still need to practice on that trick." They both laughed.

Reports went over the scanner and TV of a huge apartment fire. "It's our time." Flip said to Time. Time shook his head at Flips joke. They are standing together in the middle the basement. Flip puts his arm on Times shoulder, holding his skateboard in the other hand as Time puts the address of the building in his watch. Then they were gone.

They arrive in the back of the apartment building, 11 minutes back in time. They go through the back door, up the steps to where the apartments are in the building. They start going through the hallways, knocking on the doors, telling people to get out because the building is on fire. People are grabbing their loved ones and leaving the building. Time and Flip continue going floor to floor as fast as they can. Flip is riding his skateboard down the hall banging on the doors telling people to get out. They reach the top floor apartment. Smoke is starting to fill the building. As they are knocking on the doors of that floor, fire takes over the bottom of that stairway. Flip says, "Hurry up, get out!" Time looks at Flip and says, "Look, the stairway is blocked going down". Time tells the people to follow him as he heads up the steps towards the roof. Flip says, "Go ahead, I'll be right there. I'm going to check and make sure everyone is out on this floor". Time is on the roof with the people they rescued, looking at the door of the stairway that is filling up more and more with smoke. A second later Flip comes running through the smoke, to the roof. "The floor is clear", Flip says, "but there's no way down." He told Time. Fire was starting to come out of the sides of the building, smoke is everywhere. Flip asks, "What do we do, there's no way out". The people gather in a circle, crying and screaming for help. Time looks down at his watch. There are only two minutes left on his timer before they must go back to the present. Knowing they can't leave these people he looks over at the building next-door. He looks at his watch and thinks for a moment, then stands up fast and yells, "It's not a Time travel device, it's a transport device!" Flip looked at him like he was crazy and said, "What?" Time runs over to the edge of the building and starts to re-calculate stuff on his watch with only a minute left. "Time, what is going on." said Flip. "I'll explain it to you later. Gather everyone together and hold hands." Time shoots his new cable out of his watch to the top of the building straight across from them. With the 20 people holding hands with them, Time hits the button on his watch and instantly they disappear and reappear on the roof of the building next-door. Everyone was just looking at each other in amazement as they saw the building where they were just seconds ago. Time and Flip step away from the people they just rescued. All of them were looking at Time and Flip wondering what just happened, but happy to be alive. Flip put his hand on Time's shoulder and Time re-calculates his watch just in before time ran out. Then they were gone, and the people stood there in wonder. What just happened? Feeling relieved and happy, they run down the steps of the building to safety, still in awe of what had happened.

Time and Flip arrived back at the basement of the garage relieved, and exhausted, about what just happened. Which is just what Flip wanted to know. Flip asked Time, "What just happened?" "We had it all wrong," Time said, "the crust off the pebble is not a time travelling device. It is for transporting from one place to the other. That's why when you try to go back in time farther than 11 minutes, it's not stable." Flip says laughing, "I guess your brain thinks differently on the edge of death!". "I guess so!" Time says.

Chapter 9
New Evil Arises

Meanwhile, at the mental hospital where Scarlet is being held, she's walking down the hallway in handcuffs with a security officer named, Samuel. He is big and muscular and not genuinely nice. "Go in, Miss Hanson, and sit down." he said. Scarlet goes in and sits down, and her doctor comes in for their daily meeting. "That would be all guard, thank you." the doctor said, and the security guard went outside and shut the door. He left a crack in it so he could hear them talk as he stood outside. What people don't know is, Samuel is a thief. He and his brother, Isaac have been robbing people since they were kids. His younger brother has been caught several times, but he has not. His brother is not the brightest, but he is loyal to his older brother, the security guard. As he is standing outside listening to Scarlet, because of the crazy stories that she has been telling the doctor, he is hoping to find out more about what she has been telling her. The doctor asked Scarlet how she was feeling today and if she feels like the medicine is helping. Scarlet replies, "yes, my mind feels clearer now". "Great!" the doctor said, "I want to go back and talk about those boys that you say just appear and disappear".

Scarlet said, "It's Okay. What about it?" "Do you still think that the boys can do that?" the doctor asked. "Yes." Scarlet said. "But you know that can't happen." said the doctor. Scarlet pushes the table in anger towards the doctor and stands up, screaming, "It did happen!" and the security guard ran in toward her. Scarlet put her hand up, saying sorry and sitting back down. The security guard asked the doctor if she was okay, she said she was, so he went back outside the door to continue listening to their conversation. "Okay, Scarlet tell me about those boys again and what you think was happening." "Okay, but I have already told you several times." "I know just please tell me again." the doctor said.

"Okay, at first it was just one boy. I would set a fire and it seems like he would know I was doing it because right after it started, he would show up and put it out. Then later, it was two of them doing the same thing. Every time I would light a fire before it would get too big, they would come and put it out, and the day I was arrested they showed up before I even started the fire. What do you think? Maybe it was just your self-conscience in the form of two boys, telling you not to start these fires." Scarlet started to get mad, she grabbed a table, gripping it tightly she said in a calm voice, "No, they were there."

"Guard, come in we are done for the day. Okay, Scarlet, stand up." the guard said. "It's time to go back to your room". The doctor tells the guard, "I will let the nurse know to up her medicine. The guard leads Scarlet down the hall. "So, these boys show up every time you start a fire?" asked the guard. "Yes, most of the time." she said. leaving the room, the guard said, "Sleep tight, Miss Hanson."

A little bit later the security guards shift ends, and he is picked up by his brother in front of the hospital. He comes out with a smile on his face. "Why are you so happy brother?" "I think I found a new way to rob a bank without ever getting caught. Let's head to the log cabin outside of the city." "For what?" his brother Isaac said, "There's nothing out there." "To start a fire", Samuel said.

Chapter 10
The Kidnapping

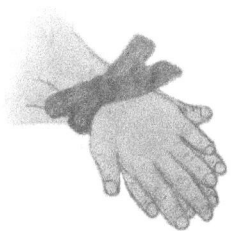

It's 6:00 AM. Jake's alarm goes off and he jumps out of bed. He heads down the hallway to the kitchen where his dad has breakfast sitting on the table. His dad asks' "Did you have a late night working in the garage?" "Yes", Jake said, "I was trying to get caught up on some of my gadgets I am making". As they were talking, the tv was playing in the background. The news was talking about the apartment building that caught fire. They were doing interviews with the people that were rescued. The twenty people Time and Flip rescued were just saying there were two boys with their faces covered telling them to get out of the building and taking them to the roof and somehow seconds later they were all on the building next to the one that was on fire no one could explain why or how. Just that these two boys saved their lives. Jeff, Jake's dad said "It's great that these two boys saved those people's lives, but I think it should be left to the professionals. Someone's going to get hunt one of these days". Jake did not say anything he just kept on eating his breakfast. A moment later, Jake asks his dad, "Do you know what happened to the man that used to live here? The astronaut?" "Not a lot. Some people in town said that he was driving his vehicle and lost control of it and drove it into the creek. But they could never find his body. The officials think it was washed away with high waters. Why are you asking?" Jake said, "I was just wondering?" "Speaking of high waters, there are tornado warnings and storms for tonight and tomorrow. I have to work a 24-hour shift at the fire department running dispatch, so be careful. Stay inside as much as you can. Do you have any plans for today and this evening?" "Not much." Jake said, "Probably just working in the garage and hanging out with Flip." "Okay, you two behave. I have to go. Let me know if you need anything." Jeff rolls out of the kitchen and goes to his truck and leaves.

Later that afternoon, about lunchtime, Jake was in the kitchen cleaning up. Outside storms have started. There was a lot of lightning and wind. There was a loud bang on the door, "Hurry, let me in!" he heard from outside. He went to the door and it was Flip, soaking wet. "What's going on Time, just trying to stay dry!" said Time, "I'm going down to the garage and into the basement, I have a change of clothes there." Time said "Okay, I'll be down in a minute".

A few moments later Flip was in the basement of the garage. Time comes down the ladder. "Look Time," pointing at the TV breaking news just came out with reports of a fire in the forest outside of the city. I wrote down the location." Flip said. "Okay." Time said as he grabbed his stuff. They both stood in the middle of the room. Time put the location in that Flip gave him and then they were gone. They arrived in the woods and they looked around and saw a cabin with smoke coming out of it. They did not see anyone around. "That looks strange." Flip says as they run towards the cabin and go inside. When they got inside, they saw an old stove. It looks like a grease fire. They look around the cabin to try to find something to smother the flames. The flames are getting bigger. Time found a jar of flour. He pours it on the grease fire. Then Flip finds a lid to the iron skillet and puts it on the fire. "Good job, Flip." said Time. As he said this, the front door slammed shut and they turned around to see there were two men standing there. It was the security guard, Samuel from the mental hospital where Scarlet is, and his brother. His brother was standing there with a shotgun pointing at the boys. The security guard said, "Miss

Hanson isn't crazy". "Flip said, "No, she is." The security guard told Flip to shut up and then walked over to pull off Flips' hoodie and Times' goggles. "How did you appear like that?" Time says, "I'm not telling you!" The younger brother takes the gun and points it at Flip. "Okay!" Time says, "I'll tell you, just put the gun down." "Tell me now." the security guard said. Time tells him, "I have a device in my watch that lets us go back and forth in time and transport from one place to another". As he is saying this, the timer goes off on Times watch. Time and Flip look at each other, then Flip puts his hand on Times shoulder. The security guard saw this and knew something was going to happen. So, he grabbed hold of Time with one hand, then grabbed his brother with the other hand. In a flash, they were gone. All 4 of them appeared in the garage. The other two men were a little confused. Time and Flip took that moment and tried to escape up the ladder. Isaac lowered the shotgun and said, Stop! Not so fast boys". The security guard grabbed the boys and threw them in a corner. "What just happened? Where are we?" "In my basement." Time said. "I told you. We can transport from one place to another." With a great big smile on the security guards face he said, "This is amazing, you boys are going to make me rich!" "Me too, right?" the younger brother said. "Of course." the security guard said.

The two men step away from Time and Flip to discuss their plan in private. Time and Flip are asking each other, "What are we going to do?" Flip said, "Right now, whatever they say.

They have a gun." The security guard
walks towards Time and Flip. "You!"
The Samuel said pointing at Time.
"So, you can send us anywhere we
want to go?" the security guard
asked. "Yes." Time said, "only if you
promise to let us go". "But of course,
you make me rich I'll let you two go".
Time says, "I just need the location."
The man writes down the address of
the big bank in the city and he hands it
to Time. Then he tells his brother stay
here watch the other boy meaning
Flip. Time said, "No, we all go."
Samuel yelled, "No, I'm in charge!
They stay here to make sure you don't
try any funny business. If you get me
what I want, my brother will set him
free, I promise." "Okay." Time says as
he moves to the center of the room
and puts the address of the bank in
his watch. He sets his watch to

transport, not Time travel. Then he puts his hand on the arm of the security guard. He says to Flip, "There's good in her." Then he pushes enter and they're gone. Time and the security guard arrive outside, next to the bank, in an alley. Samuel looked around. He grabbed Time and picked him up off the ground. "What is this?" he said. "I could drive up here we need to be in the bank, what are you trying to pull" "Okay," Time said. He looked around, then recalculated his watch. In a flash they were gone, reappearing right in the bank vault. The security guard said, "This is more like it." And drops Time to the floor. He had a big smile on his face and just laughed while putting money in a trash bag he had in his pocket. After filling the bag with money, he grabs Time telling him to send them back to the cabin. Time puts the location in his watch and hits enter and they were back at the cabin. The security guard keeps a hold of Time, so he won't try to escape. They both walk into the cabin and he pours the money onto the bed. He said, "Let's go on another trip." Time said. "Okay." And then, they were gone.

Chapter 11
Foe Becomes Ally

Back in the basement of the garage, the brother of the security guard and Flip are still there. The storm is getting worse outside. The lights are flickering, on and off. The wind is blowing the upstairs of the garage and the trees all around. Flip is tied up in the corner with Isaac standing in the middle of the floor with the shotgun. The lights flickering on and off gave Flip an idea. He scoots over to where the lights are plugged in, without Isaac noticing. Flips hands are tied, so he pulls out the plug for the lights with his feet. The lights go out. He jumps up and knocks over the shelf. It falls on top of the man, trapping him under the shelf. He tries to get up. But Flip does a tuck and roll towards him and kicks him in the head, knocking him out. Flip crawls on the ground and plugs the lights back in. He finds pliers and cuts his hands loose. When Time told him 'She has good in her' he knew exactly what he was talking about. Scarlet. He ties the man up, pulls him to the corner, and duct tapes his mouth. Flip looks around the room, thinking about how he's going to save Time. He sees the old chair in the corner. He goes and sets it and the old table up. Then he hooks the cables to the chair and the table

with the map scanner on it.
Connecting it to the new computers,
he remembers watching Time doing
this many times. He sets the
computers to transport instead of
time travel. Flip digs in the ground
to get the box that the pebble is in.
Then gets the pebble and puts a
drop of water on it. After the crust
grew on it, he took it off and put it in
the glass dish hooked to the chair.
He takes the pebble and puts it
back in the metal box and puts it
back in the ground. Then he put the
address of the mental hospital
where Scarlet is in the computer.
He sets the computer for five
minutes to bring the chair back to
the garage. Then sets his watch for
five minutes so he won't miss his
ride. He grabs Times' bag of
gadgets. He hits enter and jumps in

the chair. Lights start to flicker again. Then in an instant he and the chair are gone. Flip arrives in the back of the mental hospital. He finds a bag of trash and cardboard and covers the chair with it. This way no one will find it. He rushes to the back door and pulls a device to unlock doors from Times' bag and opens the door. With it being Saturday, there are not many people at the hospital. He sneaks around and looked in the windows of each door in the hospital looking for Scarlet. Finally, he found her room and unlocked the door and went in. She looks up and says, "You put me in here!" "I need your help. My friend has been captured by some bad people. He said you would help me." "Why should I help you?" Scarlet said. Flip said,

"Because it's the right thing to do. And you know him. His name is Jake, and he needs help. His dad saved your life. Can you save his now?" Scarlet looked at the ground then looked back at Flip. "Okay, I'll do it…. Anything is better than staying here". "Do you know where they keep your sword? asked Flip. "They keep supplies down at the end of the hall." They ran down the hall and opened the door. They went in and saw a box labeled, Scarlet Hanson. All her belongings that she had when she was arrested were inside. She grabbed it and they ran down the hall and out the door to the chair. With barely a minute to spare, they grab hold of the chair and transport back to the garage basement. Back in the basement now, Scarlet says, "So, that's how you have been getting to the fires so fast!" Flip smiles. She starts to look around. "Is that the guy?" She asked as she pointed at the man tied up in a corner. Flip said, "Yes, one of them." He's starting to wake up. Scarlet walks over towards him and pulls her sword out. Flips eyes get big. She turns the sword around and hits him in the head knocking him back out. Flip runs over and says, "Rule number one: no one dies." Scarlet turns to him and smiles. "Got it." She said. "I think they have Time at a cabin." Flip says, "Help me drag this man to the chair." Scarlet and Flip drag the guards' brother to the chair and tie him up. Then Flip puts in the address of the cabin. He asks Scarlet, "Are you ready for a battle?" she said, "Always." They grabbed the chair, and they were gone. By this time, it was starting to get dark, and the wind and rain was picking up at the cabin. They arrive outside of the cabin. Leaving the man sitting, tied up to the chair, they run into the cabin but do not see anyone. They saw a pile of money on the bed. "They must be at the bank right now." Scarlet said. "Let's go outside and wait for them to get back".

Chapter 12
The Storm Begins

As they were waiting, Flip says to Scarlet, "I hope we find them. With everything going on, I forgot to set a time to go back to the basement in the chair. So, if we do not find them, we will need a way back". Scarlet says, "How do y'all do this?" Flip answered, "It's a long story." At that moment, they saw a light in the cabin. Scarlet stays outside, Flip runs toward the door. Scarlet lights a small bottle on fire and throws it into the cabin, right over Flip's head, almost hitting him. He turns and looks at her. She rolls her shoulder and says, "Heads up!" as the bottle goes flying into the cabin and explodes in fire. Then Scarlet pulls out her sword, as Flip runs in to the cabin. The security guard looks at the fire as it gets bigger and lets go of Time. The firebomb landed right next to the bed where his money was laying. It all went up in flames. "NO!" he yells, "No, my money!" Samuel grabs Time by the shirt saying, "Your boys burnt all my money. You will pay!" Flip is next to the door and Time is pulling away from the security guard. He is typing something in his watch as he is trying to get away. He slips his watch off and throws it to the security guard. Samuel lets go of Time to catch the watch. Flip helps him pull away from Samuel and they run out of the door. Samuel puts the watch in his pocket and grabs a chainsaw and starts it and starts to run after Time and Flip. Meanwhile, outside, the security guards brother breaks loose from the ties and chair and breaks the chair by kicking it and the dish that the crust is in goes flying off. It lands in the mud. Scarlet is standing nearby looking towards the cabin. The security guards brother grabs a leg of the chair and puts it around Scarlets' neck holding her tight. He surprised her because her focus was on the cabin, she throws her neck back, hitting him in the nose with her head. He instantly lets go. When he does, she turns around and kicks him in the head knocking him to the ground. He starts to get up, but then Scarlet points her sword at him and says, "Stay." he lays back down and Scarlet said, "Good doggie". By that time, Time and Flip run out of the cabin with the security guard chasing them with the saw in his hand. Scarlet stands in front of the boys with her sword. As he comes towards her, a beep goes off on Times watch, inside Samuel's pocket. As he gets to Scarlet he looks down at the noise and disappears. Scarlet turns around to Time and says,

"What happened? "He has my watch, I set it to go back in time. I was in a hurry. I am not sure how long I set it for. We've got to go!" Time says. Flip says. "We have no way back." Time points down the road. "Let's go this way, it must lead somewhere." They start running down the road. After running for about twenty minutes, it starts pouring down rain. They are all soaking wet and are seeing nothing but woods on both sides of the road. "Stop, I need to take a break." said Time. They stopped. Then they noticed headlights coming from the direction of the cabin at a fast speed. Time said, "Good, some help." But as it gets closer,

Scarlet sees who it is and says, "No, it's not help. It's them in a pickup truck." As she says this, the truck gets closer, and they all jump out of the way. Flip and Time jump to one side and Scarlet jumps to the other. The truck barely missing them. Scarlet landed in the mud and the boys land next to the woods. The truck stops fast. Samuel was in the back of the truck and jumps out screaming and yelling in pain. His face is deformed, and the chainsaw is now connected to his arm. Flip said, "What happened to him?" Time said, "Oh no, I must have set the watch to go back in time too long. He is deformed." Scarlet stands up with mud all over her, angrily pulling her sword out, running towards the security guard telling Time and Flip to run. Samuel yelled to his brother, "Get out, go get those boys, I'll take care of her!" Isaac jumped out of the truck, running after Time and Flip. Scarlet swings her sword at the security guard saying, "Ready to go, Sawman?" and he blocks it with his chainsaw arm. Then Scarlet kicks him in the stomach knocking him down to one knee. He looks at the ground then looks up, seeing Scarlet running into the woods. He follows her, throwing his arm with the chainsaw connected to it, all over the place, hitting trees and knocking limbs down. "Where are you lady?" A voice comes from behind him. "Right here, Sawman." she says as she throws a firebomb towards his head that she got out of her bag. He ducks, and it misses him hitting the trees. It catches the trees on fire. She runs toward him, doing a flying kick in the air. She hit, him knocking him to the ground. As she walks over to him, he grabs her foot knocking her down to the ground. Now the woods are fully engulfed in flames. Time and Flip are still hiding from Isaac. He says, "Where are you boys? I won't hurt you two." Thick smoke starts to fill the woods, making it hard for him to see. Flip yells, "Hey!" and the guy looks up in the air.

Flip is in a tree. He jumps down onto his head putting him in a headlock. Time comes out from behind a tree with a log. He hits him in the legs, knocking him to the ground. Then Flip holds him in the headlock until he is knocked out. They leave him and run back toward the road. The flames get worse, and the smoke covers the area. Scarlet is on the ground. She rolls away from the security guard, just as he tries to hit her with the saw. **He missed, hitting the** ground instead. She jumps up and disappears into the smoke saying, "Come and get me, Sawman!" He went into the smoke saying, "where are you!" Trees that are on fire start to fall around the area. Scarlet comes out of the smoke behind him, hitting him in the head with the handle of her sword. She knocked him out as she said, "You are lucky we have rule number one!"

She bends down and takes Times' watch out of his pocket, then runs back to the road to meet Time and Flip. Time says, "Where is the other guy?" Scarlet says, "Sawman is taking a nap". Then she throws Time his watch. He sees it in the air and says, "Now we can go home!" It was only as he caught it that the disappointment set in, he realized, it was broken. Scarlet runs towards the security guards' truck and said, "Let's

go boys, we're going home."
They jump in the truck. Scarlet
says, "Where are we heading,
Time?" "My house." he says
and gives her the directions.
They arrive at the end of
Times' driveway. Time says to
Scarlet, "Thank you for your
help, we would be dead if it
was not for you." "What about
the mental hospital?" Scarlet
asked. "I don't know how you
escaped," said Time. "Just stay
real." Flip said, as they smile
and jump out of the truck. They
wave goodbye as she takes off
up the road.

Chapter 13
The Past Comes Back to Life

Meanwhile back on the alien planet. The human is down on his knees, bent over in pain and exhaustion from being electrocuted so many times. he told the aliens everything he knew and who he was. The NASA astronaut. He was not washed away with the creek, as was thought. He was captured by the aliens when they ran his car off into the creek. He has been on their planet ever since. He told them everything he knew about NASA and his discovery of the pebble, even where he kept it. The new king told his brother to get the armies ready. A few minutes later, the king walks to the window and looks at thousands of his people lining up, getting ready to save the planet and take all the water from the earth. The troops are holding what looks like guns, waiting for orders from the king.

The aliens do something similar to what Time does with the crust from the pebble, but much more advanced. They put the crust in their weapons and a device hooked to them so they can transport. They do not know how to go back in time. The astronaut did not tell them about that discovery. The younger brother walks into the room and says, "The troops are about ready king. How are we going to get them to earth? We do not have enough crust to get the whole army to earth." The king walks to a corner and picks up a long staff with a round end on it saying, "Leave it to me, brother." They walked together to where they have the astronaut. He is banging on the glass and screaming. Sparks of electricity **are** coming from his fingers with his veins glowing in green. He is still in a lot of pain and he is cracking the glass. It appears he has gone crazy from eels being connected to him. They open the glass tube he is in and water fills it up. The guards come in to help hold him down. In the struggle, he shoots electricity out of his fingers, hitting one of the guards and knocking him out. They finally overtake him because he could not breathe in the water. They put a mask on him so he would survive. The King walks over, hitting him in the head with the end of the staff. He knocked him out. The brother grabbed him dragging him next to the king. He has hold of the astronaut and is putting one hand on the Kings shoulder. Using the device connected to the king's body, they disappear and transport to earth. They arrive in an alley, in the middle of the city, dropping the astronaut in the middle of the road. The alien king says, "Welcome home, Astroshock, the humans are going to get a shock out of you!". Then, laughing, the king and his brother transport again.

Chapter 14
The Fall

    With it still storming, Time and Flip run to the basement of the garage. Time says to Flip, "This is not what I want." "What do you mean?" Flip says. "I want to help people. Today, people just got hurt." Flip said, "Well we do good also." "A little bit of good," Times says, "doesn't make up for the pain of others". Time turns off all the equipment in the basement.

Then goes to the ladder. They walk toward the house, with it still storming awfully bad. Time takes off his watch and throws it into the woods… "Why did you do that, Time?" said Flip. "I'm done. I don't want anyone else to get hurt." Flip says, "Okay, I hope you change your mind." and walks towards his house.

Time goes to close the garage door and turns around to a big surprise. It was the two alien brothers. The younger brother pushes Time into the side of the garage. He points a weapon at him and fires the weapon. Shooting past Time and hitting the garage. It caused the whole garage and everything in it to disappear. This made Time fall back into the hole where the garage was sitting over the basement. It knocked him out. The younger brother alien jumps to the ground of the basement, digs in the floor and pulls out the metal box where they kept the pebble. He grabbed the box and jumped out of the hole. Then they transported back to their planet without saying a word and with it still pouring down rain and storming.

The hole Time is in begins to fill up with water. With Time knocked out he's going to drown. Lights flash at the top of the hole and someone slides down through the mud, to the bottom of the basement. They grabbed Time and dragged him out of the hole to safety. A few days later Flip comes to Times house to check on him, then sees the garage gone and takes off running to the house, knocking on the door. Times dad answers, "Where is

Jake? Is he ok?" Flip says, "Yes." his dad says, "High winds or a tornado must have hit the garage. When I got home, Jake was in a hole where the garage was. I crawled down and got him out and did CPR on him. Because Jeff used to be a firefighter, he has very strong upper body strength. Even though he was paralyzed, he was still able to climb down the hole and back out to save Jake. He is good now. He is resting in his room. I knew the storm was bad and he was not answering the phone, so I came home and good thing I did." "Yes, for sure!" Flip said. "Can I see him?" "Sure." said his dad. Flip walks to the door of his room, knocking. "Yes?" Jake said. "It's Flip." He says as he walks into the room. He shuts the door behind him saying, "What happened?" "It's all gone." Jake says.

Thinking he means the garage and all the stuff in the basement. Jake was laying in the bed not looking at Flip. "We can replace all that." Flip said, "No, you're not understanding. The pebble is gone. So that means we are done. We have no more crust left." Every time they use a piece of crust in their time devices it starts deteriorating. Without the pebble, they can't make any more. Flip thinks to himself, how did the pebble blow away, underground in the basement. He starts to ask another question, but Jake stops him and says, "Please go away." and turns to the wall. Knowing he is hurt and tired he starts to leave but first he puts his hand in his pocket and pulls out Times watch and puts it on the table next to his bed. Flip picked it up after he threw it in the woods the other night. Flip walks out and shuts the door to Jake's room. He walked through the house and said goodbye to Jake's dad, "I'll be back in a few days to check on him." "Okay." He said.

Chapter 15
Astroshock Comes Home

Flip walks outside and hears a horn beeping at the end of the driveway non-stop. Flip runs down to see who it was, and it was Scarlet. "What are you doing?" Flip said to her. Have you all not seen the news?" "No, what?" "Some old man is blowing up police cars and a whole block with his hands and something that strange must involve you guys." She says laughing. "So, let's go stop him."

"Okay!" said Flip, as he jumps into the truck. "Just you?" said Scarlet. "Yes", said Flip. "Time is under the weather." They speed off to the city.

To Be Continued